life lessons

je rowney

the lessons of a student midwife

BOOK ONE

Also by this author

Charcoal
Derelict
Ghosted

Copyright © 2020 JE Rowney

All rights reserved. This book or parts thereof may not be reproduced in any form, stored in any retrieval system, or transmitted in any form by any means—electronic, mechanical, photocopy, recording, or otherwise—without prior written permission of the publisher.

This is a work of fiction. Names, characters, businesses, places, events, locales, and incidents are either the products of the author's imagination or used in a fictitious manner. Any resemblance to actual persons, living or dead, or actual events is purely coincidental.

Chapter One

Tangiers Court is unexceptional, but I can hardly contain myself when we reach the front door. Number twenty-one. Our new home.

"So, this is it."

I look at Zoe, and she looks back at me. I'm trying to keep a straight face, and contain my excitement, but my best friend has already completely lost it.

"This is definitely it." Zoe pushes her key into the lock and pauses for dramatic suspense, looking at me with a huge grin on her face. "Ready?"

I nod, no longer even trying to hide my emotions. I can't. We have both waited far too long for this. She reaches her other hand down to take hold of mine while turns the key.

"Well…" she says.

She's in front of me; I can't see into the house, into our house.

"Is it okay? Let me see!" I nudge her slightly and she moves over.

It's a very average, ordinary hallway. The walls are magnolia, the carpet is beige and all-in-all it is unremarkable.

"I love it!" We shriek at each other and if there was enough room in this narrow space to jump around, we would definitely be doing that.

Close enough to be able to visit our parents if we want to, but far enough away to feel free. Zoe and I have arrived at our lodgings for the next year. We have finally made it to university.

"Choose rooms first or get our stuff?"

I nod towards the staircase. Zoe runs without a second thought and I'm not far behind.

We are the first to arrive at the student house, so we get the pick of the rooms. The accommodation spreads over three floors, with two bedrooms on the first floor, and two more up top. The upper rooms are converted attic areas, with slanted ceilings and not nearly as much space as the ones below.

Zoe takes one look into the higher bedrooms and screws up her nose. I smile, and we race back down to the rooms that we are about to claim as our own. The other students will have to take what's left.

The rooms are more-or-less the same size, Zoe heads into the room on the left of the landing, and I go right. It's an arbitrary decision; it's not like we would ever argue about something like this. We've been friends for far too long to fall out over anything.

Hauling our belongings out of Zoe's Corsa, along the road and up the stairs in our student house, today feels like the beginning of an epic adventure.

There was never any doubt that we would choose to go to the same university, the only doubts I had were whether I would get the grades I needed to get here. It's been a tough few years, but here I am. Wessex University. I made it. A week from now I will be embarking upon the start of my student midwife training. In three years' time I'll be a qualified midwife.

At least if I make it through the course I will.

"Are you off in your little dream world again?" Zoe says.

I've stopped because the two bags of clothes and accessories that I'm carrying are a lot heavier than I expected, but, yes, I'm also miles away, or rather years away.

"Just taking it all in," I smile. I hoist one of the bags onto my hip and start moving again.

"It's going to be so much fun living together. All the booze, boys and –"

"Books. We won't have any time for the other stuff," I say, and I almost believe myself.

"You think it's going to be back-to-back lectures and hitting the library every night?" she laughs. "You do that if you like, but my first job, as soon as we've got the rest of this," she nods at the box in her hands, "in there", she bobs her head towards the house, "is to go and find the student union bar and get absolutely…"

"Wasted," I smile.

We push back in through the front door and head up the stairs. Zoe is still laughing along with me and manages to catch the corner of the box she is carrying against the bannister. The cardboard container and its contents spill down the stairs like a landslide. I hop to the side, and barely miss being swept away by 'Wuthering Heights', 'Pride and Prejudice' and the slightly less classical, but classic all the same, 'Bridget Jones's Diary'.

"Oh pants!"

"Luckily not pants, just books." I plop my bags down on the hallway floor and start to gather up the texts for her. She teeters down to help.

"I brought way too much. You're probably right though: I don't think we will have much time to socialise. Teaching and midwifery aren't the same types of courses as say…" She pauses while she tries to think of a standard uni course. "Sociology, or, English or something. They are like five hours a week of classes. We are going to be in all day every day."

"And then some. I start my first placement next month."

"It's going to be tough, even if I don't start mine until the new year," she says.

I put the last couple of Zoe's books on top of one of my bags and carry them the rest of them for her.

"It's going to be great. Trust me. The two of us, here together. How could it not be?"

Zoe grins, then turns and makes a second attempt at carrying her stuff upstairs. This is our third trip from the car to our rooms, and we each still have a couple of suitcases to drag up. Zoe's parents offered to come and help, but saying goodbye at home felt so much easier.

My mum doesn't drive; she could have come with Zoe's folks, but I tried not to make too big a deal about me leaving. I'd rather that she thinks I am only a short distance away, and that I haven't really left her. Zoe's parents have each other, my mum and I have only had each other for the past year. At least, my dad left physically last year, but emotionally, he's been absent for as long as I can remember.

"You worrying about your mum again?"

Zoe stands in the doorway of my room, and looks in on me. I've put my cargo down and sat on the edge of my new, single bed in my new single room, and my thoughts are obviously wandering back to home. She'd know what I was thinking about even if it wasn't obvious. She's been my best friend for fifteen years, she knows everything about me, and I know everything about her.

I nod and try to cover up some of the sadness in my expression, but she can see through me. She knows. She always knows.

"It's okay," she says. She sits down on the bed next to me and puts her arm around me. "Oh, your bed is way more comfortable than mine. Feel that bounce!" She lifts her bum off the duvet and drops it back down. "Mine's like a rock."

"We can swap. I really don't mind."

"No way! You know I have a better view."

As better views go, it isn't much. I can see the street from my room, and Zoe gets to look out over the small patch of grass that the landlord called a 'communal garden' in the advert.

"Far better. Way better. I don't know what I was thinking." This is what she does, she picks me up and lifts my mood from brooding to laughing, just like that.

We have a bathroom on our floor, and there's another toilet upstairs. Whoever designed this place was definitely into their plumbing. I'm not complaining. I am a huge fan of long soaks in the bath, and I am not going to feel half as guilty about indulging knowing that anyone desperate to clean themselves or, well, whatever, can use one of the other facilities.

Downstairs there's a shower room slash toilet combo, shared galley kitchen, and a living room that could either be described as cosy or compact, depending on how much you wanted to dress it up. It seems spacious now, but once there are two more people living here, I can imagine that it might start to feel cramped.

Zoe doesn't let me wallow in my thoughts for long.

"Shall we finish off getting the stuff?" she says, "I've left the car open." As an afterthought, she adds, "And it's on the double yellows."

I nod. "Let's do it. But Zo…"

"Yeah?" She's stood up and she's reaching her hand to pull me to my feet.

"Even if we are going to spend the rest of our student lives with our heads in books, living the life of sad spinsters –"

"Less of the sad!"

"Okay, happy spinsters. Let's go out tonight. Let's celebrate being here."

She reaches her second hand out too and pulls me up and towards her into a hug.

"Absolutely. We've earned this. Let's make the most of our week before classes."

"I'll definitely drink to that!"

It takes us the best part of an hour to finish unloading and unpack our belongings into our rooms. The process is punctuated by the pair of us popping across the landing to visit each other's rooms, sharing our excitement. There's not much in my bedroom; a bed, a desk, a wardrobe. Luckily,

I don't have much to fill the space with. Clothes, books, make-up, some scented candles. Despite the fact that my best friend will be living across the hall from me, I have a photo of the two of us printed out and framed that I put at the back of my desk, next to my ceramic pen pot. Her deep red hair almost tangled in my boring brunette, her bright green eyes glowing in contrast to my muddy brown. Both of us laughing. I don't even remember the moment this photograph was taken. I can't recall what it was that was so funny, because it could have been anything. I have so many photos of the two of us like this on my phone.

She has been there for me through everything. Happy times like the ones in all those photographs, and the less happy times that I would rather forget. Before I head back into Zoe's room to help her finish up, I sit on the edge of my bed and take a moment alone. I send Mum a text to let her know that I am here, and that I am safe.

I never thought I was good enough to get to university. I struggle with exams; I struggle with self-confidence. I did it though, I made it. I always knew that I wanted to be a midwife. Not a nurse. I never wanted to be a nurse. I mean, there are a lot of similarities, but the things that are different are the things that appeal to me the most. Being with a woman during such an important, emotional experience as pregnancy, labour and the postpartum period is such an amazing privilege and honour. I never thought I would make it here though.

I'm lost in my thoughts when Zoe pops her head around the door.

"You okay?" she says.

"Yeah."

"Having a moment?"

I smile.

"I had one too." She walks in and sits on the bed next to me.

I made it this far, and with Zoe by my side I'm almost certain that I will succeed.

True to our words, when we have finished unpacking, we get ready for our first night out as university students. The main campus is a ten-minute walk from Tangiers Court, or at least it should be according to Google maps. It's starting to get dark, and there's a park to cut through, so before seven o'clock we are on our way out.

Zoe pulls open the front door and thuds directly into a tall, dark, and rather scruffy male.

"I'm sorry -"

He smiles, and she stops talking. She's standing with her mouth open, and I give her a subtle prod and shake my head.

"Zoe, be cool," I whisper into her ear.

She clears her throat.

"Can I help you?" she says in the most put-on accent I have ever heard her use. This is the face-to-face equivalent of her telephone voice.

The man tilts his head, looks at her, and then at me. I notice that he looks at her for longer, even if it is only a matter of seconds. Zoe's earlier comment about not having time for relationships pops into my head. I shake the idea away.

"I'm Luke," he says. He holds out his hand to her, and she looks at it.

"Zoe," she replies. "Can I help you?" She tentatively reaches to shake hands.

"No, it's fine, thanks. I couldn't find anywhere to park, so I wanted to check that I could get in first."

"Get in?"

A look of realisation passes over his face.

"I live here," he says. "Or at least, I am just about to."

Zoe mimes a little facepalm expression. I'm standing behind her, trying to fade into the background. She waves her hand to me and says, "This is Violet. We live here too."

"Lovely," he says.

There's an awkward pause, Luke on the outside of the doorway and Zoe firmly in the entrance. She's still staring at him. I nudge her again and she turns to me. I nod my head to the side of the door a couple of times, hoping she will catch on, and she does.

"Sorry, sorry," she says again, and steps out of Luke's way. "I'm an idiot. At least we have got that out of the way."

He actually laughs, and I see Zoe's face turn a fiery shade of red. It suits her; it blends well with her hair.

"Not at all." He steps into the hallway and shakes my hand too.

"Nice to meet you." I give him a mock-apologetic smile, and Zoe digs me in the ribs playfully. "We were about to head out to the union bar." I say it as in invitation, but Luke doesn't bite.

"I need to bring my things in, maybe unpack a little, and…" He sniffs his armpit melodramatically. "I probably need a shower."

"There's one on this floor. And a bath on the first. Your room will be one of the ones on the top floor I'm afraid," Zoe says. She's still curt and business-like.

"So, I do need a shower?" he smiles.

"I didn't…I mean…"

"I think he's messing with you," I say, and Zoe facepalms again. I love this girl so much.

"Top floor is fine for me. You two bagged first floor then?"

We both nod.

"I need the exercise anyway," he says and gently pats his stomach, which appears to be completely flat despite his intimation.

"No, you…" Zoe starts to speak and then stops herself.

"We should probably be going then," I say, linking arms with my best friend. I need to get her out of here before she says something she might regret.

"If I finish sorting everything out, I will come and find you." Luke gives us a nerdy salute, I nod, and Zoe tries to replicate his gesture.

"Later," I say, pulling Zoe out of the door.

"Yeah, see you later!" Zoe echoes.

I close the door behind us and pull Zoe into a hug.

"You're so funny," I say, my face pressed into her.

"He seems very, er, nice," she replies.

"Just remember that his room is on the top floor, and yours is on the middle. No getting lost in the night."

She laughs again, and we stand there on the doorstep of our new home, collapsing in hysterics.

This is the beginning of something special, I just know it.

Chapter Two

Four hours later, Zoe fumbles her key in the lock, and we tumble back into the house. We have learned three things tonight. Number one: gin is a pound a shot in the student union bar. Number two: it takes approximately four and a half measures of gin each to get giggly drunk. Number three: seven gins are around two too many.

"I don't feel so good," I drawl.

"I don't feel anything. Let's not do that again."

"Not tonight anyway." I wobble along the corridor and flop into the living room without turning the light on.

Zoe keeps walking, her arms outstretched to either side of her, hands on the wall, supporting her and guiding her, and maybe keeping her upright.

I sit in the darkness, trying to focus on stopping the room from spinning.

From the kitchen I hear the sound of Zoe turning on the tap and making a pained groaning noise. Despite the fact that the room feels like a roundabout that I can't keep my balance on, I get back up to my feet and stagger down the hall after her.

She's standing over the sink in what I can only describe as the 'about to chunder' position.

"Oh Zo! Hey. It's okay." I reach over her and scoop her hair back into a ponytail, holding it up, behind her, just in case. "I'm here. You're going to be alright." I'm not even sure if I am going to be alright, but I can't bear to see Zoe suffering. For the past fifteen years, it's just been the two of us. She and I have looked out for each other and have been there for each other for as long as I can remember.

Instead of heaving, she sways a little and starts to fall in my direction. I plunge my hands down to catch her, and stumble backwards a half step, knowing I am about to fall, her on top of me, me crushed and just as bleary drunk below.

But that's not what happens.

I lean back into a tall, man-shape. Zoe collapses onto me, and at my rear, our new housemate, Luke, catches us both.

"Good night was it?" He is squashed against the fridge, and although he's trying to hide his discomfort, I can tell he is straining to keep us semi-vertical. The space between the sink and the fridge isn't exactly huge, and it is definitely too small for two sprawling drunken teenage girls and one well-meaning rescuer,

"Something like that," I say, and gradually move so that Zoe slides gently to the floor. That leaves Luke and I standing, his arms looped beneath my armpits.

"Er, thanks," I mumble, and step over Zoe, out of his grasp. "Sorry."

"Kind of wish I had come out with you now. Housemate number four doesn't seem to have moved in yet though, so I don't know who would have stepped in to catch me." He has a friendly smile, and despite my deep embarrassment to have made such a bad early impression, he still manages, somehow, to make me smile back.

"We would have behaved better if we had a good influence with us."

"Yes, so I hate to imagine what would have happened if a bad influence like me had been there." He winks, but more in a joking way than flirtatious. At least, that's how I interpret it. "Have you had some water?" He steps over to the sink and pours out two tall glasses from the tap.

Zoe seems to have settled into a rather uncomfortable sleeping position on the floor. She looks like a cross between a discarded ragdoll and a starfish. I pull off my sweatshirt and tuck it under her head.

"You're okay," I whisper. "You're okay here." I think she is. She's better off horizontal here than vertical anywhere else right now. Luke and I can step over her. It's fine. I'm sure it's fine.

"She'll be fine," Luke echoes my thoughts. "Maybe get her duvet? Don't think we should move her."

"She would be mortified if she knew you had seen

her like this," I say, and then I cover my hand with my mouth. I have said too much.

"I'm sure that living together this year we are all going to see a lot of things. What happens in Tangiers Court stays in Tangiers Court."

He hands me the water and we clink glasses.

We don't repeat the excesses of that first night during the rest of Freshers' Week. I'd like to claim that we got it out of our system, but to be honest, Zoe couldn't face another morning of waking up on the kitchen floor wondering where she was and how she got there.

During that week we found out where the nearest supermarket is (five minutes in the car, no problem), joined up to several university societies that we will probably never attend (Zoe went for yoga, and I was taken in by an allotment-tending club, don't ask me why). We have also worked out where the lecture blocks for our first week's classes are. It's not a large campus, so even though Zoe and I are in separate faculties and different buildings, we won't be far apart.

Sunday night, the evening before week one of classes, I have planned to check my timetable on the online app, make sure my bag is packed with everything I will need, and pick out a cute outfit for tomorrow. I know that my cohort will be mainly female, it's a profession that is dominated by women, even though there are, of course, male midwives, I'm not trying to impress anyone. That's not my style anyway; I've only ever cared about what I like, never about what anyone else thinks. That was my plan anyway. Instead of getting ready I have been sitting on my bed for the past half an hour, my head spinning and my stomach feeling as though I have swallowed a block of ice. I can't do anything. I can't concentrate. All I can do is sit and hope that this feeling passes.

Ten more minutes pass, maybe fifteen, and I hear the thud of footsteps on the stairs. A flash of red hair whips around the doorframe and Zoe pops her head in.

"I thought you were taking a long time. You okay?"

I shake my head. I can't even speak. Not even to Zoe.

She takes a seat next to me and puts her arm around me.

"Hey. It's alright," she says.

She's seen me like this before. So many times over the years.

My anxiety started in my first year at secondary school. I was eleven years old; there was a lot going on in my life, and I guess I couldn't deal with it all. It was probably a culmination of all the stressful factors, or at least that's what my GP told my parents. School work, family life, growing up, all those things. Up until the end of primary school I was the brightest in class, and I loved it. Once I started at Kingsbury Grammar, I was back at the bottom of the pile, a newbie struggling to find my feet. My mum and dad were teetering on the brink of the divorce that would take six more years to finally happen. Add those together, sprinkle them with a dash of onset of puberty, and apparently that's the recipe for crippling anxiety. Through it all, I have had Zoe. Always.

I mutter a few words and Zoe scrunches up her face in concentration trying to decipher them.

My hands are clammy and cold, but my head feels hot and heavy.

"I can't do it," I say. Each word is painful to produce. There's a tight ball in my chest where my heart should be. I'm breathing too shallowly, too quickly. Zoe puts one hand on the centre of my back.

"Ssh. Slow it down. Slow. It's okay. You're okay."

"I'm not."

She moves her hand in a circle, stroking gently, trying to bring me down. It's like she's trying to get me on track, to realign me. It usually works, eventually.

"You will be. Hush. It's okay, Vi." She kicks out at the door, which I had left open and she in turn hadn't closed when she came in. Now it's she and I, and the rest of the world doesn't matter. I breathe in, and then exhale a shaky sigh.

"I can't do it. I really want to, and I thought I could, but I can't."

She keeps moving her hand, and she shakes her head. "It's not you saying this, it's your anxiety. You know that you can do this. You wouldn't be here, about to start university if you couldn't do this. They don't let just anyone in, you know. You passed your A-Levels, you got through the interview, and you made it." She's looking straight at me, her entire focus upon my face, watching my reactions, and trying to find the right words.

I don't have a counterargument.

"You've wanted this for as long as I have wanted to be a teacher. This has always been our dream. The two of us, here at uni together, working towards our ideal careers. We have done it. Don't pussy out on me now, Vi." She gives me a huge smile and pats my back gently. "You're going to be fine."

All I can think about is walking into that classroom tomorrow with all the other students, who are all going to be better than I am, in every way. I'm not clever enough, not good enough. I feel like a fraud. Yes, I passed my exams, but it must have been a fluke. There must have been some kind of mistake. I don't deserve to be here.

My breathing rate has increased again, and Zoe frowns at me.

"Really. Come on. Don't let your brain do this to you. Don't let your anxiety spoil this moment for you." I close my eyes and concentrate on regulating my inhalations, slowing down, exhaling deeply. "That's it," she says.

When my parents were fighting, when they divorced, when I had a hopeless crush on the boy I sat next to in maths class, just so I could let him copy off me, when I thought I would never pass my GCSEs, when I thought I shouldn't have gotten into college, when I split up with Jared, my first boyfriend, my first love, when I was certain that A Level biology was going to destroy me…all of those times and so many more, Zoe was there for me.

I suck breath in so sharply that I feel the kick in the back of my throat.

"That's it." She pulls me in towards her and wraps both arms around me in that familiar comforting hug.

"I'm sorry," I say. "I'm such an idiot."

"No, no, no," she says, stroking my hair. "Your brain is an idiot sometimes, that's all. You'll show it though. You can do this, and you will do this."

I wish it was as easy as believing her and believing in myself. It isn't. The feelings that have been brewing within me will continue to bubble, but

I can't let them take over. Not now.

We sit for a while in a silent embrace. I listen to her heartbeat thud against my ear and feel her warmth. The only sound is our breathing, we don't need anything else.

Chapter Three

Monday morning, the first day of term; my stomach is churning. I barely slept last night, and when I did, I had dreams that I had missed my alarm bleeper. My mind is buzzing, so I get up at seven, rather than trying to get back to sleep and I sit at my desk, reading through the course pages on my laptop.

There are six weeks of lectures before we get let loose in the community. By let loose, I mean that we are each assigned to an experienced community midwife, who will guide us gently into the first stages of our 'hands-on' training. The community teams provide antenatal care in clinics, sometimes in the hospital, and sometimes in women's homes. They do postnatal visits, and sometimes intrapartum care and delivery. It's possible to experience nearly every facet of maternity care during the community placement, so it's a great place to start. Like I said, that's six weeks away, and that six weeks feels like forever.

My timetable shows an induction session at nine o'clock in the lecture block. Zoe isn't starting until nine thirty, but she's heading in with me. I'm leaving it to her to work out where the best place on campus is to get coffee.

"Good luck, Vi," she says, pulling me into a huge hug.

"Oh Zo, I can't believe we are really here."

"Knock 'em dead," she says. Then she pulls back out of the embrace to give me the kind of grin that only she can. "Not literally, obviously."

"Zoe!" I tap her shoulder in a playful gesture. "Not even funny."

"Go. Go on, you'll be late."

"Good luck too."

I smile, I nod, and I head to the lecture block for my first day as a student midwife.

By the time I get to the classroom, the world feels like it is moving in slow motion. It doesn't seem real. It's as though I am a character, stepping into a dramatisation of someone else's life.

I always try to sit somewhere in the middle of a class. At the front it feels too confrontational and exposed. I don't want the lecturer to direct every question at me; I don't have the confidence to give answers when I know so little. At the back I wouldn't feel engaged enough in the class. I want to be a part of it, but not too much so. I guess that sums me up. I take a seat next to the wall about half-way down the room. Everyone here so far is dotted about in isolation. There are no identifiable friend groups yet. This is the beginning; we all have a clean slate.

I pull my notebook and pen case out of my bag and place them neatly on the table in front of me. I love stationery, and I was glad to have the excuse to pick out new goodies to bring with me. Having these treats makes me feel a little more relaxed. I focus upon my floral pencil case, rather than letting myself get lost in my negative thoughts. I am so focussed that I don't notice when a girl with a short blonde bob and floral dress sits herself down next to me. It's only when I finally look up that I realise she is there.

"Oh hi," I say.

She nods, and I'm sure she's almost trembling. She looks how I feel. I guess I have had a long time to perfect not letting my anxiety show through in public.

"Hi," she says, in a soft, quiet voice. "I'm Sophie."

"Violet," I say. "So many people. Scary, isn't it?"

She smiles a little and looks away. I give her a moment, and she turns back.

"It's all a bit surreal. I can't believe I am finally here." So, I'm not the only one. It's always a relief to know that whatever anxieties I have, that I am not alone in my thoughts.

"Same," I say. "I can't wait to get started."

There are twenty-two of us gathered in the classroom by the time the lecturer arrives. She is a short, round woman with wild curly hair. Her shirt is a bright purple Batik print, which she has paired with leggings and oxblood boots. Somehow, she looks exactly as I would have imagined a midwifery lecturer to look. I suppose we all look exactly like students, which evens the score. She drops her bag onto the chair at the front of the room and stands next to the lectern. We lower our chat to a polite silence, and she begins to speak.

"Welcome to your first day as future midwives."

An excited hum passes through the room as everyone turns toward the strangers sitting to either side of them, beginning to build shared bonds.

The lecturer lets us have this moment and pauses before continuing.

"I'm Zita Somerville, Programme Lead for Midwifery Studies. I'm also the module leader for the anatomy and physiology class you'll be taking this term. I am going to tell you, right now, on this very first day: this is not an easy course." We all start to mumble to each other again, but this time she carries on. "You will learn all of the theory that you need to know to enter the workforce as skilled novice practitioners, but," she pauses again, for effect this time, "the real learning will take place when you are with women."

She turns and writes the words 'with woman' onto the whiteboard. The marker pen squeaks against the board as she forms the two words that give the literal definition of midwife. Mid- wife: with woman.

"In France, we would be called a sage-femme,

which means 'wise woman'. In days gone by we would have been called witches. I know what I prefer. With woman. That is what this, your vocation, is all about: being with a woman. Supporting her. Being by her side throughout the most intimate, emotional, challenging period of her life."

"What about men?" a male voice says from the left of the room.

"Simon, hello," the lecturer says. "The role of the midwife goes far beyond simply caring for a woman, and you will learn a lot about relationships, sociology psychology…a little bit of law, and a lot of ethics. You'll need communication skills, diplomacy, mathematics…"

There's a small but noticeable groan at the mention of this, and a laugh in response from the rest of the group.

"I'll be sure to keep an eye on you when you're calculating your drug administration," the lecturer smiles. "We have a role in protecting and promoting the health of communities. You may have days when you feel more like a social worker than a midwife. This job will make immense demands upon you." She pauses again. "You will rise to the challenge, and you will succeed. You will succeed for every woman and baby, for every husband…" Another pause. "Or wife." She is working the crowd well.

"So, Simon, you are going to be a male midwife, and yes, you will support the women and you will do that by supporting their wider family, by identifying their individual needs, and by doing everything you can for them. When you can't do any more, or when you yourself need support, you will find it, and you will build your own toolkit. You will never stop learning. The three years that you are here are merely the beginning of the journey."

Sophie has been scribbling in her notepad the whole time that Zita has been talking. When the speech is over, she finally looks up from the paper, and smiles at me.

"Inspirational," she says. "I feel a bit better now."

"It's going to be a lot of hard work." I'm fired up by Zita's words too, but there is so much to this course, so much to learn.

Sophie tilts her head slightly and looks at me. For a moment I wish I hadn't said anything. I don't want other people thinking that I can't do this. I feel terribly vulnerable until she puts her hand on mine and says, "It is. But we are all in it together now."

I break into a huge smile and let go of a wave of tension within me that I didn't even realise I was holding. Looking around the room, I can see the same shared looks, whispered words and the seeds being sown of support, of friendships, of a real community.

At the front of the classroom, Zita sits in silence and watches.

"This is a three-year course, and it is a marathon, not a sprint. Remember that. You are not going to do everything all at once. You have walked in here today as novices, but you will learn and develop throughout your three years, gradually and steadily. When you complete your course, you will continue to learn. Every day that you practice as a midwife, for the rest of your careers, you will continue to learn. You will never know everything."

This also feels like a relief. When I think about how much I need to learn it makes me nauseated. The impossibility of knowing everything is terrifying, but of course nobody can know everything. I like Zita. She knows what to say. She is realistic. She is keeping us grounded.

She clicks on the computer and brings up a copy of our practice documents on the display screen. A copy for each of us is circulated around the room. I receive my heavy coil bound A4 slab and place it on the desk in front of me. It stares at me intimidatingly.

"In your placements, you will work on completing the competencies required to pass the practical elements of the course. Everything is set out in your PAD, your Practice Assessment Document. Make sure you read it carefully. Your placement mentors will support you to make the most of your experiences."

I browse through the list of competencies that run over page after page. I start to feel dizzy thinking about the huge amount of work that this will entail. There is one list that grabs my attention.

Advising of pregnant women, involving at least 100 antenatal examinations

Supervising and caring for at least 40 women in labour

Performance of episiotomy and initiation into suturing

Personally carrying out at least 40 births

Supervising and caring for 40 women at risk during pregnancy, labour or the postnatal period

Supervising and caring for (including examination) at least 100 postnatal women and at least 100 healthy newborn infants

Active participation with breech births (may be simulated)

Observation and care of the newborn requiring special care, including those born pre-term, post-term, underweight or ill

Half of my time will be spent in university, and half on placement. Wondering how I am going to manage to fit in all those activities makes my head spin.

Zita is still talking.

"Try not to worry too much about getting

everything done," she says, as if reading my mind. "I guarantee that the students who graduated this year all had the same thoughts when they were sitting where you are now. Every one of them achieved their competencies with time to spare."

"They weren't me," I say quietly.

"You'll be fine," Sophie says. "Really. It's going to be okay. We can do this."

I try to smile, but the words and numbers on the page stare up at me accusingly. She's trying to reassure herself as much as she is attempting to comfort me though, I can tell by the way that her fingers tremble slightly as she flicks through her pages.

"Read through the module guides. Familiarise yourself with your PADs. The sooner you start filling in your competencies the better. You don't want to be starting your final year thinking that you have time to complete eighty more antenatal checks, or you're going to find yourself struggling."

A hundred antenatal checks. A hundred postnatal checks. Forty births.

The room feels so hot and stuffy, I need to get outside. I need to breathe. I don't think I can sit here for the rest of this session. The heat is rushing through me like a tsunami. My cheeks are burning, my palms are sweaty, I'm going to…

"Violet? Violet?

Sophie is tapping on my arm, her voice getting louder. I snap myself back into the room.

"Ugh, I'm okay. Thanks." I'm not okay. Not really. My head is still swimming. I need some fresh air. The clock shows we only have five minutes left of the lecture; I think I can make it.

"Are you alright, Violet?" Zita calls over from the front of the room.

"Uh, yeah. Just hot, sorry."

She nods and flicks a button on the desk. "Air con should kick in shortly, give it a minute. Just let me know, anyone, if you need more air, more light, anything, okay? These are going to be long days, and I want you all to be comfortable." She looks back over to me to check that I am alright, and I give a feeble nod in return.

I'm going to have to get a grip on myself; I can't carry on like this every day. I consciously measure my breaths and tell myself to keep it together.

At the end of the session, I stuff my book into my bag, relieved that the class is over. We have an hour and a half until the next introductory slot. I text Zoe.

What time do you get out of there? xx

She replies almost immediately.

Noon. How was it? xx

It's eleven thirty now.

Exciting! Where are we meeting? xx

Again, her reply is rapid.

Bradley's. Back of the library xx

I'm still standing in the classroom, tapping away at my phone. Everyone has left apart from Zita. She walks down the aisle to the door and stops to talk to me.

"Are you really alright, Violet?" she says.

No point in hiding anything from her. Maybe being honest and open will help.

"I get anxiety attacks," I tell her. "I'm mostly used to them, I mean, you know, they are awful, but I have had them for a few years now. Sometimes," I shrug, "they overpower me a bit."

"Sounds tough, I'm sorry. Well, if you ever need to leave the room, you just walk out and take a breather. We can always have a catch-up afterwards if you need to. Let your mentors know too." She tugs in her bag, pulls out a leaflet and hands it to me. Student Support Services. "Give them a call, or pop in. They are really good."

"Thanks." I have had all kinds of support before, and nothing has helped to eradicate my anxiety. "I appreciate that."

"And talk to Deb Cross, she'll be your link tutor. She's lovely."

I smile. "Thanks."

We walk to the door together, and I slip the leaflet into my bag.

"How did you find it, apart from," she waves her

hand instead of completing the sentence.

"I'm looking forward to getting stuck in. I can't wait."

We smile at each other, and head in our separate directions.

Bradley's is a small, strange shaped building tagged onto the back of the library. The counter area and its glass-fronted unit, brimming with cakes and sandwiches almost fills one end of the room. The rest of the space spreads out towards tall windows, comfortably allowing around a dozen round tables. We haven't discovered anywhere better on campus yet, so this, for now, is us.

I don't have to wait long for Zoe. She gets her usual extra shot, extra hot mocha and drops into the seat next to me.

"Sheesh!" she says. "You should see the size of our practice portfolios. There's so much paperwork!"

"Same." I nod to my bag, which is being held open by the A4 coil-bound PAD. "And I nearly had a full-on anxiety attack so that was, er, fun."

She puts her hand onto my shoulder, almost instinctively.

"Nearly? Are you okay now?"

"I think I was a bit overwhelmed by it all. There's so much to do and I…I don't know if I can do it."

She's about to speak, and I raise my hand to stop her. "I know. You don't have to say it. It's just my stupid brain making me feel like this."

She rubs on the place where her hand sits upon me.

"You remember that, Vi. Next time your brain starts being a dick to you. Promise you'll remember that."

I nod and take a sip of my drink. I feel a lot more relaxed now. This place is ideal, Zoe did well. It's quiet. We can talk here. I can think.

"So, tell me about your morning," I say, and we chat, animatedly and excitedly, full of optimism for the future until the end of our break.

Chapter Four

I settle into lectures far more easily than I expected. I have a regular pattern of classes, with Wednesday afternoons off. That's when the academic staff have all of their meetings, and we can get stuck into the social groups that we signed up for in Fresher's Week. Zoe has managed to go to two yoga classes, but I haven't stepped foot on an allotment. I have a slight suspicion that I may have been drawn to sign up by the vaguely attractive student behind the stall, rather than any real green-fingered aspirations.

By the end of the first month, the upstairs room at Tangiers Court has remained mysteriously empty. When Zoe and I agreed the lease on the rooms, we were told that there would be two male students moving in with us, but only Luke has arrived. It means that we have a little extra fridge space, more room in the cupboards, and that I can take a bath pretty much any time I want to without feeling bad for blocking the room. It also means that we have invented a fourth housemate.

"Who's left this mug and plate in the sink again?" I shout through to the living room.

"Must be Andrew," Luke replies.

"Oh, of course." I laugh and clean them for him. "Whose turn is it to buy milk?"

"Um, I think it's Andrew's," says Zoe.

Luke heads down the road to the corner shop and comes back with a communal pint of semi-skimmed.

Basically, Andrew has become the scapegoat for anything any of us want to avoid doing. Don't get me wrong, on the whole, we are working well as a mini team. Despite his sometimes reluctance to wash up behind himself (he says it's because he never had to at home) Luke is fairly handy around the place. He's the only one who hoovers, and I am sure that it is Luke who is responsible for squirting green stuff into the toilets on a semi-regular basis. Either that or it's Andrew.

Luckily, we pay rent for each individual room rather than having to split the rent for the house between three of us rather than four, so Andrew's absence is a blessing rather than an inconvenience.

Today it's Andrew's turn to make dinner, so we end up ordering takeaway.

"How's your course going, Luke?" Zoe asks, reaching over for another fried chicken ball.

"Mmm-mm," Luke nods through his mouthful of crispy chili beef.

"Enlightening, thank you," she laughs.

"Do you have any lectures at all?" I ask. "I'm basically in Monday to Friday, and Zoe seems to live between lectures and library now."

He's studying accountancy, which seems to mean he has approximately two lectures per week. Either that or it seems that way because Zoe and I have such full timetables.

"Bah, you get Wednesday afternoons off, just like everyone else," he laughs.

"I never see you go to uni though."

"Don't you worry, Miss Violet. I fully intend on getting the education that I am going to be spending the next ten years of my life paying for."

"And the rest!" Zoe says.

"Maybe you'll have to find yourself a rich husband to pay off your student loan then," Luke smiles, and plucks the final spring roll off Zoe's plate.

"Oi!" she says, thrusting her chopsticks towards him playfully.

He raises his eyebrows.

"Fight me for it. Chopsticks versus chopsticks."

"Alright, settle down!" I say, but they don't hear me; they are having a bizarre fencing match with the wooden implements. I shake my head and twirl my noodles.

"Yes!" Zoe shouts. I don't think there were any set rules for the chopstick battle, but Zoe is claiming victory.

"A fair fight. Well won," Luke says. "You can have Andrew's spring roll."

"I'm sure it was mine," Zoe says. Still, she pulls it apart and splits it half each with him.

"Very sporting of you. Thanks ma'am." He stuffs it into his mouth, and Zoe eats her portion just as greedily.

"I think it was Andrew's turn to wash up," I say, as we finish up the last of the meal.

Zoe raises her eyebrows and shakes her head at me.

"You might want to check the rota there, Vi," she says. I know it's my turn. At least there's no cutlery to wash today. I gather the plates, and Zoe starts to stack the takeaway cartons.

"Thanks mate," Luke says. He leans back in his chair, stretching, and his t-shirt rides up exposing a slightly flabby, furry belly. I look away, but I notice that Zoe does just the opposite. She catches my glance and her face prickles red.

"Go and pick us a film to watch," I suggest as I head to the sink.

Luke lets out a belch.

"Lovely," I call back. Zoe laughs, and pulls him into the living room.

Chapter Five

One of the worst parts of studying is group work. There's something about being thrown together with people that I don't really know yet and being expected to create something fantastic that fills me with dread. Worse still, the fantastic thing that we have to create is my worst nightmare: a presentation.

It might not seem like something that I should be afraid of. Getting up and talking in front of a class of twenty or so like-minded classmates is hardly wrestling a pit of angry snakes, scaling a tall building without a safety harness or plucking a spider out of the shower because Zoe has been screaming at it for the past five minutes. I'd rather do any of those things than give a presentation. Preparing a PowerPoint is fine. I can do the groundwork, pull everything together and make it look perfect with pretty pictures and detailed diagrams. Stand me up in front of a class though, and I turn to jelly.

Ironically, this module is colloquially known as 'FUN' – the Fundamentals of Midwifery Practice. As you can imagine from the name, it's meant to lay out the basics that we need to prepare us to step into our practice placements. Each week we will be given a topic to read up on, do our research in a group and then feed back to our course mates. Each week. Yes. Once every week, I will go through this trauma. On the upside, the other part of this module will involve skills lab sessions where we can get some hands-on experience – albeit on each other and on mannequins.

It makes sense that the lecturers want to know that we are safe and knowledgeable about the basics before we are launched into our community placements, but surely there must be another way. Even without my anxiety attacks I can't imagine that I would ever enjoy public speaking. Is it really public if it's the closed confines of the classroom? It's far too public for my liking, I know that much.

I enjoy working alone. I like to get an assignment, focus all my attention and energy onto it at my own pace, make my own decisions. I want everything to be perfect, or as perfect as I can make it, every time. I don't know if I can count on other people, other students that I barely know, to put in the work. Group work. Presentations. Ugh.

We've been part of a class together for four weeks, and the only person I have had the chance to talk to at any length is Sophie. I mean I suppose I could have made more of an effort, but we have sat together during every class so far, and everyone rushes off in their own directions, with their own little groups, during break times. Of course, I go to find Zoe; perhaps it is my fault that I don't know my course mates better.

The lecturer has thrown us into groups rather than leaving us to choose for ourselves, but luckily, she did it according to where we were sitting in the classroom. I'll be with Sophie, and the two students that were sitting on our row at the time: Simon and Ashley.

Today's morning session was a lecture on antenatal physiology; this afternoon we are starting our group work. Each group has to describe one aspect of the physiological changes experienced during pregnancy. Our topic is 'describe the effects of placental hormones on the woman's body'. We have to use articles, textbooks, and the internet to pull together all of the information to present to the rest of the class. After lunch, we gather in one of the small, dark study rooms in the library. It's a quiet place to get our thoughts together, close to the resources that we will need.

"I hate this," is what I want to say. Instead, I take a seat and smile at my group buddies. "Where shall we start?"

We spend a couple of hours picking out the key points. Ashley has an artistic eye, so she types everything into the PowerPoint, and adds a few appropriate images. Simon has the sharp suggestion of adding all our blurb into the notes section.

"If we forget anything when we're presenting at least it will all be there."

It sounds like a great idea, but the very mention of the word 'presenting' sends chills through me. I know that we are drafting a document that we will use as a presentation, but I've tried to dissociate from that fact. I'm trying to see it as gathering information with the team, trying to make sure that we have covered all the bases. I've pushed the thought of having to stand up and make a presentation to the corner of my mind. If I pushed it any further, I might be able to drop it out of reality. I can't though. I know I can't.

"Do you want to run through it?" Simon asks, as Ashley saves the file to our shared drive.

Sophie and Ashley both nod enthusiastically. Whatever the opposite of that is, that's what I do. I'm silently, steadfastly unenthusiastic.

"You don't think we need to?" Simon's voice isn't unfriendly. I think he has misjudged my fear for overconfidence.

"I should have probably mentioned this sooner," I say, "but I hate presentations." I put my hands over my face and rub at my eyes. "Ugh. I'm not very good at being in front of people. I don't deal well with pressure." I drop my hands and look Simon in the eye. "I have terrible anxiety attacks." I shrug.

There's no other way of saying it. "I don't think I can do it."

Sophie smiles at me and says, "We can do the talking. You've done your share of the work, it's okay."

I'm about to accept with a whoosh of heartfelt appreciation, but Simon is shaking his head.

"It's better for you to try to get used to this now. We have presentations every week this term while we are in uni. You're not going to be able to skip it every time."

Sophie opens her mouth to cut in, but Simon raises a hand to silence her.

"Really. It's a good skill to learn, and you can do it. When we are in practice we are going to have to talk to a lot of people about a lot of difficult things. Being able to articulate our thoughts and explain things clearly is crucial."

The explanation makes sense. I don't get the feeling that he wants to be mean. I would still rather sit it out and let these three do the presentation instead though. I can already feel the blood thudding in my temples, and the familiar knot has tangled itself in my stomach. I don't even know if I can run through a practice presentation in front of these three.

"We are here, okay? We are a team now," Ashley's voice is so soft and calming. She is going to be amazing at talking to women when we get out into practice. Everything about her tone fills me with confidence. "Try. Okay? Just try this week. Try this time. We all know all of the presentation, so if you need to sit out, you nod at one of us and we will take over for you." She looks at Simon, and says, "This time. As long as you promise to try."

"I know that anxiety attacks are awful, Vi," Sophie says. "My sister has them, and I've seen how hard they are. We aren't going to push you. We want to help."

My mind is flipping between grateful thanks for their support and abject fear at the thought of stepping out of my comfort zone. These three people who hardly know me are prepared to step up to give me the time and support that I need so that I can do the best that I can do. That means a lot to me. I can't let them down.

I nod timidly.

"Okay?" Simon says.

I force a more resolute nod, and he smiles.

"Phew." He relaxes. "I'm not good at being firm like that. I thought I might have pushed it too far." He laughs, and I relax enough to join in. "You can do it though, Violet. You've got this."

"Sure. I've got this."

They don't make me stand up to do the run through. I sit in my seat and click through my section of the slides. We've split it between the four of us, so there's not actually that much for me to present. Three slides. That's all I have to get through. Just three slides.

As soon as I start to speak aloud, I feel like I have lost control of my mouth. It's like I am chewing a huge ball of gum. My tongue won't form the sounds. My lips flap, my cheeks glow. I shake my head.

"Sorry, guys," I say.

How can I not even be able to do this? I'll never have the confidence to stand in front of class if I can't sit with three people.

"It's okay," Ashley says. "Be calm."

I want to say that I would love to be calm, but that's rather difficult when I'm on the edge of an anxiety attack. I don't. I give a weak smile and read the words on the screen silently to myself.

"Tell you what, we will pop out for a minute, so you can practice on your own. Read it out to yourself. Get familiar with it. Alright?" Simon seems to know a lot about dealing with what I am going through; this sounds like a good idea.

"Sure," I say. "Thanks."

They leave the study room, Sophie patting my arm supportively on the way past, and I am left alone.

I'm too hot, my breathing is too fast, the words are spinning around my head. Be calm, be calm, be calm. I repeat it to myself, slowly and gently, trying to get a grip on my feelings.

One final deep breath in and out, and I focus my attention onto the laptop screen. I can do this. I must learn how to do this. I can do this. I'm going to have to stand up in class, so I get to my feet. I imagine the rest of the cohort there in front of me, all interested in what I have to say. Focus. Focus. Think only of the words, the explanation, the presentation.

I start to speak. I let the text on the screen guide me as I describe antenatal blood volume changes, and how they affect the pregnant woman. I start off stiff, trying to hold my body still, trying to keep it under control. By the end of my section, I am loose, gesticulating at the screen with my arms, almost relaxed into the moment.

When I come to a stop, I look over to my right and see the three of them in the doorway.

"That was perfect," Simon says. "I knew you could do it."

"Brilliant," Ashley nods. "I think you even added some things on that I missed from the slides. You were spot on."

Sophie grins and claps. "Awesome!"

I feel like I have achieved something, like I have taken the first steps. I have to repeat this in front of the class though, and that thought still terrifies me.

Chapter Six

Zoe doesn't start her placements until February and she barely has any practice time this year compared to me. I feel a little bad for her, because I'm finding it difficult to stop myself from enthusing about my rapidly approaching community visits. I love my course, I love our home, and I love university life.

I'm not sure that I am having the same experience of university as my course mates. Living with Zoe makes a difference. We live within a bubble here at Tangiers Court. Zoe and I haven't spent much time in the student union bar since we arrived. Not that the first night and the sickness that ensued put us off completely, I suppose it is more that Zoe and I are already a tight unit. If I was here on my own without her, I might feel the need to socialise, to go out to the bar, to actually attend the clubs I joined during Fresher's Week, but instead, most of our spare time is spent self-contained within the sphere of our friendship.

Some nights Luke stays at Tangiers Court with us, and he fits neatly into our group. Not like a puzzle piece that we were missing, more like a bolt-on, an optional extra. The house is comfortable and even more spacious with the ongoing absence of our fourth housemate; we definitely got lucky with our residence.

Thursday night, the evening before my presentation, what I should be doing is sitting in my room running through my lines like an actress going up for her big-time audition. I should practice and repeat until what I am going to say is fixed in my mind, and I have no room for self-doubt anymore. If I can recite it by rote, I don't need to feel anxious about it, that's my reasoning anyway. Still, even the thought of this starts familiar prickles of panic.

I say that's what I should be doing, because it is not what I am actually doing. Instead, I am sitting at a table in the student union bar with Zoe, Luke and three lads that I have never met before, but who are, apparently, Luke's best friends. The occasion that persuaded me to leave my books and come to the union, despite my presentation? It's Luke's birthday. He invited us, and I really couldn't say no, so here I am. 'Bros before presentations' doesn't work quite as well as I would like, but the sentiment is there.

Ten o'clock and two hours into our session, I am pacing myself well. Instead of the usual gin and tonic that Zoe is still throwing back, I have switched to diet cola, with a gin every third round. Surprisingly, this has still led to me feeling lightheaded and on the cusp of inebriation. Luke's friends are from his accountancy course. Damon, blonde, not yet over his teenage acne and from somewhere up North by the sounds of his accent. Rajesh, who must be at least six and a half feet tall and swears like a docker. Florin, who has a strong Eastern European twang to his voice, which is becoming more pronounced the more lager he drinks. Apparently, these guys are who Luke spends his time with when he is not with us.

I don't want to appear impolite, with it being Luke's birthday, but I have my phone on the table, and I keep glancing at the time.

"Have to be somewhere?" Florin asks.

I shake my head. His breath is thick with alcohol, and he has to lean in far too close towards me to make his voice audible over the noise of the bar. He's dangling precariously over the pint glasses on the wooden table between us.

"No. I have a thing tomorrow." I don't feel like explaining further, but I don't have to. He sits back up as Rajesh announces that it's Damon's turn to go to the bar.

Zoe is nestled on the opposite side of the table from me, in between Luke and Florin. I was sitting next to her, where Flo is now, but I popped to the toilet about half an hour ago and there was a change around. I don't mind too much. I'm on a stool, facing the three of them. If I want to say anything to Zoe, I have to shout over to her. This is another reason why we haven't really spent much time in the student union bar – neither of us particularly enjoy it.

From where I am sitting, I can't hear what Zoe and Luke are saying, but he leans in to speak into her ear, and she smiles in response; they switch so that she can reply.

Would it be rude for me to pick up my phone and refresh myself on my presentation? I can read through the notes here. It wouldn't take long, and…

Before I can even reach over for my phone, let alone open it, and start to read, Rajesh plops himself down onto the stool next to me.

"How's your course going?" he says. Standard conversation at the union bar.

"Yes, fine, thanks." I'm not one for small talk, and my mouth dries up just as the conversation does.

There's a heavy silence, or as near as there can be to a silence in a bar as loud as this, then he speaks again.

"Luke says you're going to be a midwife."

I think for a second before answering. This can go one of two ways. I can give him the short, sharp answer, or I can start to enthuse about my life dreams and how I can't wait to start my placement. He's drunk, and only being polite. I love talking about my course, but now isn't the time.

"Yes." I hope I don't find it as painful to talk to the women that I meet on my placements. I am terrible at this. I never know what to say. I either say too much or too little.

This is why I find it hard to make friends.

This is why I hardly ever go anywhere.

This is why, or one of the reasons why, it has always just been me and Zoe.

I don't think it is the two gins that are making my head spin. I need to get outside; I need some air. My throat. My mouth. Everything has dried up. I feel like my airway is clamping shut. I flash my eyes at Zoe, but she is still leaning in towards Luke, deep in conversation. I need to get out of here now. I think I'm going to –

There's a man in a black shirt and trouser combo standing over me. I can just about see the badge that shows he is campus security as the room starts to come back into focus. It's still loud, too loud, but it's not as busy anymore, at least not around me. There's a bare circle radiating out from where I am lying on the floor. I am the epicentre. I have clearly thrown everyone out of my path with some previously unknown superpower. Either that or the more likely explanation: security have cleared people back from where I am splayed out to keep them from treading on me.

Damon is still sitting on the opposite side of the table. Luke and Zoe are to either side of me; Zoe is squatted on the floor by my head, and Luke is standing to my other side, talking to the security guy.

"I don't think she needs a first aider," I hear him saying. "She's coming round. She's going to be fine." He leans down to me. "Are you okay?"

I use all the energy I can muster to nod.

Zoe bats away a student that walks past, leaning in too closely to me. "Get out of it. It's not a performance. Get lost." She strokes my hair away from my face. "Maybe the bar wasn't a good idea tonight," she says. "Let's go home."

I frown. "You…stay…with Luke." I sound pathetic, trying to push the words out, but my brain feels like mushy peas. Did I really only drink two gins? Two singles? I was feeling fine. I've not left my glass all night, so I know there's no chance that it's been spiked. I must have lost count, either that or I had doubles instead of singles and, well, the end result is this. Anxiety plus alcohol is not a good cocktail.

"I'm not leaving you here," Zoe says. I knew that she would insist on coming home with me.

"Really, get…" I take a deep breath. "Get a taxi and I'll go home to bed. Probably for the best anyway." The words are coming more easily now. I need to get back to Tangiers Court though.

"No way." Luke says from above. "We are getting you home. No argument."

"Luke, no. You stay with the lads. It's your birthday," Zoe says. "We will be fine. I mean I will be fine with Vi, and she will be fine."

Luke is resolute. I see him turn to his three friends, and although I can't hear what he says to them from here, I can see the disappointed expressions on their faces. I have a deep sinking feeling. Violet the party-killer. I ruin everything. My anxiety ruins everything. I should probably stay away from other humans that are trying to have a good time.

Zoe is on the phone now, calling a cab, making the arrangements to get me home. I want to sit up, get back on the stool and carry on the evening like a normal person, but as soon as I start to move, I want to vomit.

Luke kneels to my left. "Hey. Do you want me to carry you?" From his earnest expression, I can tell that he is completely genuine in his offer. I can't accept though, even if my whole body would be grateful for the excuse not to expend any energy right now.

"No thanks. But thanks. Really. And you don't have to leave. Zoe will look after me." Just like she does every time. It must be draining to be my friend sometimes. Here she is, having drinks like any normal student would do, and her stupid friend has to go and balls it up.

My father was right. I always make a mess of everything I do. I always bring down anyone that I spend time with. I'm a waste of space. That's all I am.

Zoe has stood up, and I can see her exchanging worried glances with Luke. I've ruined his birthday. I've ruined her night. That's what I do. I ruin everything. Tomorrow I am going to mess up my presentation. The room is getting dark.

"Violet!" Zoe reaches down and places her hand on my forehead. "She's clammy."

The security guard repeats his suggestion of getting the first aider, but I am with it enough to be able to shake my head.

"She has panic attacks," Zoe tells him. "She will be alright in a few minutes. Honestly."

I do need air though. I need air and I need my bed.

Zoe looks at her phone and then at Luke. "The taxi is here," she says.

Luke reaches down and hooks his arms beneath my armpits. I haven't had my moving and handling training yet, but I am fairly sure this isn't standard. He pulls me to my feet, slowly and gently, and looks at me for a few moments, assessing me.

"Can you walk?" he asks.

I step forward, and then take another step. I feel woozy, but I'm going to make it to the street.

"Good," he says. "Sorry to cut it short, guys,"

he tells his friends. "We'll have a double session at weekend to make up for it."

"It's not your birthday then, so we won't have to buy your drinks," Rajesh says. He's sitting back at the table, Damon has come back from the bar with their drinks, and it looks like the three of them will be fine without us.

"Fair enough," Luke says with a smile.

"I'm sorry." I look at Luke and try to hold back unexpected tears.

"Hey. It's fine."

"Oh Vi." Zoe slips her arm around me and guides me towards the door. The crowd parts to let us through and I feel the weight of everyone's eyes upon us. They probably think I'm just another silly girl who can't handle her drink. I wish that were the case.

Chapter Seven

I had planned to leave the party early and get home in time to run through my presentation. I did leave early, that's for sure.

I mustn't have set my alarm for this morning, because Zoe comes in to give me a shake awake.

"Eight o'clock, dozy duck. How's your head?"

It's too bright, too loud. I want to stay asleep. I pull the covers over my face in protest.

"Come on," Zoe says, not taking my avoidance for an answer. When I don't reply the second time, she tugs the covers down to look at me. "Are you alright to go in today?"

This is the perfect excuse for me to duck out of the presentation. I can send my apologies, explain, and everything will be fine. I give her a bleary-eyed groan.

"We should have stuck to singles," she says. "Sorry."

I know really that a hangover is not a good enough reason to miss class. I'm surprised the drink hit me so hard, but it has been a while. Add to that the whole anxious anticipation of today; I suppose my body is trying hard, but my brain can't quite handle it.

I hate myself right now. I knew I should have stayed at home and prepped for the presentation. I have three full hours in the skills lab this morning, no time at all to run through my lines. Maybe Zoe will listen to me over lunch. The thought of food starts to make me feel nauseated. Today is not a day for breakfast. It is, however, a day for wearing my student uniform. That is one tiny shred of positivity in the puddle that is my day ahead: the skills lab practice is my first actual opportunity to wear my uniform outside of the confines of my home.

Despite feeling rotten and terrified by the prospect of this afternoon, the skills lab session does manage to excite me a little. The atmosphere in the corridor as we wait for the lecturer to arrive is filled with an excited buzz.

We are all dressed in the grey tunic, navy trouser combinations of our student midwife uniforms. Of course I have stood in front of the mirror back at Tangiers Court, admiring myself, staring at my reflection in disbelief that I have made it this far.

Rather than taking away our individuality, wearing these uniforms only serves to unite us as a group. We have an identity and a shared purpose. We are working together to achieve our own individual and joint goals.

As I chat to my classmates my hangover starts to settle. My anxiety is still there, lying in wait, but it's a distant rumble rather than a deafening noise now.

"Feels kind of weird," Sophie says. Her eyes are sparkling, and I can tell she feels the same buzz that I do.

"Good weird," I say. "Here, let's get a selfie before Zita arrives." I angle my phone, and she leans in toward me, face gleaming in a natural smile. "Perfect!"

I know that I will be wearing this outfit here for these sessions, and out on my placements, many times over the next three years. Today, dressed like this for the first time with the rest of my cohort, the thrill makes my heart hiccup.

Zita Somerville arrives bang on time and unlocks the door to let us in.

"Don't you all look fabulous in your uniforms?" she says as she pushes the door open.

The skills lab is a large room, set out in part like a hospital ward, and in part like a clinical suite. The walls are white, the wall-mounted cupboards are white; the strip lights on the ceiling cast a harsh glare onto every surface. There are three hospital beds, each with the same kind of faux-wooden over-the-bed tables and side cabinets that I would expect to see in a real ward. There is even a nurse call bell, along with an emergency buzzer by each of the beds.

To the other side of the room is a platform with an overhead heater, and a plastic goldfish bowl type unit that I understand to be a hospital crib.

Everything about this room is exactly what I expect I will find in the wards, when I finally get there. The only things missing are the patients.

"Today you will be practicing your skills on each other," the lecturer says. "We are going to run through the standard physical assessments that you are likely to perform regularly as midwives. Blood pressure, pulse, urinalysis." She pauses. "And then we will try out some abdominal palpation on our simulation models."

It's almost enough to make me forget about the presentation that I am going to have to give this afternoon. Almost.

"Into pairs, please." She does a quick head count to make sure there are an even number of us. I'm next to Sophie, so the two of us work together.

Somerville runs us through what we need to do, but when I try to listen to Sophie's blood pressure, I hear nothing. I watch the needle on the dial skip from a hundred and eighty, down through all the numbers to zero without catching any noise.

I shrug.

"Sorry, you don't have a blood pressure," I laugh.

Sophie grins. "Did you find the right place on my arm to listen in to?"

"I guess not. Shall I get Zita to show us?"

"No, let me help you." Sophie presses her index and middle finger onto the bend in her arm, and then guides my hand. "Here."

I place the end of the stethoscope onto the spot where my fingers meet her skin, and I try again.

This time, I hear the dull thud, thud, thud of her heartbeat. I am so impressed that I have found it that I almost forget that I am meant to be watching the dial as the marker moves.

"Fit and healthy. Sounds great. Thanks, Soph."

She smiles, and then we swap over.

She checks my pulse first, two fingers on my wrist palpating my radial artery. Her eyes focus on the clock as she counts.

"Is your heart rate always this fast?" she asks.

I thought I was calm and in control. If my anxiety was making my pulse quicken before, it must be even faster now that she has mentioned it.

"Is it bad?"

"I was only joking." She smiles, and I try to smile back. "Hey, really, it's fine. You're worried about this afternoon?"

"Yeah. I feel like I am going to let everyone down."

"Impossible," she says. "It's the first presentation for all of us. We are all in this together. Look around. Everyone is doing new, scary things."

She waves her arm around the lab. In pairs, in every available space, my classmates are trying to put into practice the new skills that we are all starting to learn. None of them look fazed by it; everyone is helping each other.

"Maybe my blood pressure will be too high, and you'll have to send me home." I try to find something humorous to throw back to her.

She puts the stethoscope in place and listens carefully.

"You're fine," she says. "Perfect."

I shrug. "Good news is I have perfect blood pressure; bad news is I guess I have to stay for the presentation."

Zoe lets me read my presentation to her over and over while she drinks her mocha and eats a sandwich. I manage a latte, but I can't bear the thought of food. I still feel that woozy mix of nervous energy and last night's borderline excesses.

"Does it sound right?" I ask, as I finish my fifth run-through.

She shrugs. "I have no idea if what you are saying is correct, but you make it sound as if it is. I don't know the first thing about oestrogen and progesterone, apart from the fact that I hate it when I get PMT and one of those hormones is probably to blame."

I smile through my haze of anxiety.

"Something like that. Thanks for listening. I know I am probably boring you."

"Not at all! I'm always happy to help. Besides, by the end of your course I will probably learn a lot about pregnancy and birth too."

She gives me a final good luck hug as I drag my feet up to the afternoon's classroom and prepare myself for the moment of doom.

We sit in our workgroups, and chat while we wait for Zita. My lines were fresh in my mind when I walked into the room, but as soon as we start to talk, I feel them fading away.

Simon is talking about something completely unrelated to the presentation, and part of me is grateful for the distraction. A larger part of me can't think about anything else.

"Good afternoon," says the lecturer "How did you all get on with your workgroups?"

There's a mass hum of responses before Zita indicates a girl in the front of the class.

"It was interesting looking things up. I think we found it useful to help us learn."

It was. I can't disagree. I like the research side of study, finding out new information, pulling it all together.

"Simon?" she asks.

He looks at the three of us before speaking. "I just want to get the presentation out of the way," he says.

There's a quiet burst of laughter throughout the

class.

"Would you like to go first?"

He looks at us again. Do I want to get it over with, or put it off for as long as possible? I think I am going to be sick. My empty stomach tumbles like a washing machine. I nod.

"Sure," he says. "Let's get it out of the way."

The lecturer smiles. "I used to feel the same about presentations when I was a student," she says. "And now I'm doing this. It gets easier. I promise." She addresses the class. "I want you to take notes, and if you have any questions, wait until the end of the presentation, alright? Remember it will be you up here next, so lots of support and no talking during the presentations."

Collective heads bob up and down.

Simon gets up first and walks over to the computer stand. He taps on the keys and brings up the presentation. I didn't even think to email it or bring a memory stick so it's a good job someone was focussed enough to do the practical things. I try to get to my feet as Ashley and Soph go to join him. That swimming feeling in my gut threatens to turn to a drowning feeling. Sophie reaches out her hand to me.

"Let's do this," she says. Her voice is full of confidence and warmth.

"Okay," I say. My voice is quiet, uncertain, and

timid. I clear my throat and repeat. "Okay."

"That's it." Sophie holds my hand, literally and metaphorically.

We walk to the lectern, and the four of us stand, ready to give our presentation. Looking out into the classroom, I see only supportive faces. I take a deep breath, let it out, repeat, and begin.

It's nowhere near as bad as I had expected. In fact, it all passes by so quickly that we are sitting down again before I know it, ready to watch the other groups.

Sophie pats my arm.

"That was great, well done."

"Thanks. I didn't stop to think. When I was up there with the three of you, it felt like I switched to autopilot."

Zita shoots us a look from the front of the room and puts her finger to her lips. The next group are taking their place at the lectern. On the outside I give the impression of focussing all my attention on the speakers, but inside all I can think about it the warm glow that is filling me, knowing that I did it. I gave my two-minutes-worth of presentation without messing up or falling flat.

Zoe is waiting outside the lecture block for me when I tumble out at the end of the afternoon.

"So how did it go?" she asks, looping her arm into mine.

"Apart from the part where I said pic-turitary instead of pituitary, it was fine."

"Well, it's an easy enough mistake to make," she says. "Not as bad as you thought then?"

"I don't think anything could have been as bad as I thought that presentation was going to be. Even if I had my dress tucked into my knickers, it wouldn't have come anywhere close to as bad as I imagined it. I'm an idiot, aren't I?"

"You're not an idiot. You have anxiety. Sometimes anxiety has you. Anxiety is the idiot. I'm glad you got the better of it today. Maybe this is the beginning of you kicking its arse?"

"I hope so!" One small victory is a tiny step towards winning the war. My anxiety has been a part of me for so long that I can't begin to hope that one success means that I will overcome it, but today feels good. I feel good. Perhaps I really can do this.

Chapter Eight

Tangiers Court isn't exactly the most spacious of homes, even with the absence of Andrew. Still, when Luke asks whether it's okay for him to invite Florin, Rajesh, and Damon over, Zoe and I don't think twice before agreeing.

"We're going to have a poker night," he says. "You two are welcome to join in."

"I've never played before," I say. "I'm sure I would be terrible at it."

"It's not strip poker, is it?" Zoe grins. "I want to know what I am getting myself in for if I say yes."

"With those three? You think I want to see them strip?" He lets out a sharp laugh. "I don't think so. It's just a bit of fun. Damon has some cards and chips."

I pop my head out of the living room and look towards the kitchen.

"I guess the table is big enough," I say, despite having no idea how much space we would need to play poker. It's a card game. How difficult can it be?

"And will you be expecting us to provide the refreshments?" Zoe has a lot of questions, but I think we have both already made up our minds to join in.

"We are going to order pizza and have a few beers," Luke says. "So, is this okay with you two? We can go to Rajesh's if you –"

"No, it's fine," Zoe says, quickly. "Sounds like fun. Vi?"

"Sure. As long as there's no real money at stake, count me in!"

I have time to read up on the basics before Friday night, when Luke plans to host his game night. Maybe Zoe and I can even have a little bit of a practice. We haven't had houseguests since we moved in, and it seems like a good opportunity to show Luke's friends that I am not always falling on the floor drunk.

By Friday evening, Zoe and I have watched three YouTube videos and had a hilarious heads-up practice session. We are, as I predicted, terrible poker players.

Despite Zoe's show of not wanting to be responsible for the refreshments, she has been to the supermarket to gather a range of snacky foods and a bottle of gin for the two of us. Considering my resolve to show myself in a different light tonight, I should really not drink too much of that. Damon came back from uni with Luke and they are up in Luke's room, probably discussing tactics.

Zoe is emptying bags of crisps into little bowls, busying her way around the kitchen. I pop a cheese puff into my mouth.

"Do you need any help? Might just stick to the

diet Coke tonight, Zo."

"Keep a clear head for the game?" she says, batting my hand away from the dishes.

"Something like that." I back off and sit down at the table.

Luke has laid out a green felt cloth from Damon's poker set. It's like a tablecloth but marked with a line across the middle for placing the community cards. I've learned something this week, at least. We all get two cards, and then others get dealt onto the table. Whoever has the best hand wins – unless someone bluffs, that is. I am a horrendous liar, so I am hoping for good hands.

When she has finished prepping the snacks, Zoe pulls me upstairs so we can both get changed. It's game night at home but, as we don't get out much, it's more than enough of an excuse to make a little effort. She puts on some subtle make up and runs the straighteners through her usually wavy hair. I manage some mascara and a swish of lip-gloss and throw on a plain green tea dress.

Rajesh and Florin arrive together at just gone half past eight. Rajesh is playing the part with a Vegas t-shirt and one of those plastic visor-headbands. Florin has his sunglasses on top of his head. Luke and Damon have come down to join us in the kitchen and are both on their second cans of lager by the time the other guys arrive.

"Hey! Grab some snacks, come and take a seat," Luke says.

We gather around the table, Damon slides a stack of chips to each of us, and we are ready to begin.

It doesn't take long for everyone else to see that poker really isn't my game. Every time I see a pretty card (one of the ones with a picture instead of a number) I put chips into the pot. Apparently, this is not a good strategy. Rajesh and Damon both have some previous experience of playing, by the looks of their stacks. They keep scooping the pots towards them, whilst Zoe and I see our stacks shrinking with every hand we play.

By the time the pizza has arrived, I am already out, but I don't mind too much that I get to sit on the side lines and watch. Zoe has a lucky double-up when she puts all of her chips in with a pair of eights ("my lucky number") and gets lucky against Florin's pair of Kings. I chew on a slice of ham and mushroom and try to follow the game.

From where I am sitting, I can see both Luke's cards and Zoe's. He peels up the corner of his carefully, trying not to reveal them to anyone else, but I am at the right angle to be able to see them anyway. Zoe lifts her hand up so haphazardly I'm sure that any of the guys would be able to see them if they wanted to. So far, they are being very sportsmanlike and avoiding looking at what she has.

Zoe is down to her last few chips. Luke is by far the chip leader. He has most of the chips that I started with, as well as a fair proportion of everyone else's. There's no prize for winning apart from bragging rights, but he is certainly giving it his all.

Zoe lifts her cards to show two Jacks. Two picture cards has to be a good hand, I know that much. She looks at the others, and says, "I raise".

"How much, Zo?" Luke asks. He has been prompting her gently throughout the game, in a helpful rather than condescending way.

"Ten," she says. It looks like she has about sixty-pretend-dollars of chips left. If she doesn't win this one, she's probably going to be out.

"Okay," Luke says. "Ten dollars from the lady. Florin, it's on you."

Florin shakes his head and pushes his cards forward.

"Not for me," Rajesh says, folding his hand.

Luke hasn't looked at his cards yet, or at least I haven't seen them.

Damon is in the small blind position; he already has one-pretend-dollar in the pot. "Not with this rubbish," he says, and lets his hand go.

I lean slightly to see Luke's cards as he peels up the corners.

A red ace.

And another red ace.

I may not know much about poker, but I know this is not good news for Zoe.

Luke clears his throat in the worst example of not giving away any information about his hand that I can imagine.

"How many chips have you got left there, Zoe?" he asks.

She puts her hands up as a barrier around her stack, shielding them from his view.

"You can't have them. I have a very good hand. I think you should fold. The other guys have done exactly the right thing. I'm not bluffing."

She is deadly serious, but it's obvious that she is trying hard not to let any emotion show through in her words.

Luke smiles. "I know you're not bluffing, but I am going to have to raise you," he says. "How much do you have?"

Zoe makes a show of looking behind her hands. "Not many. Not enough for you to worry about. I have sixty dollars total. Ten there in the pot and fifty here. I could buy something nice with these pretend dollars. A new pretend bag, or maybe a pretend dress."

We all laugh, but I know that Zoe is in trouble here. She's not going to be pretend buying anything.

"I'm going to make it thirty dollars." Luke counts

out the chips and puts them onto the green felt.

"Thirty dollars? That's half of what I've got left."

"That's quite right," Luke says. "You're on the wrong course. You should definitely come over to accountancy with us."

Zoe raises her eyebrows. "I don't think so, mister. Are you trying to bully me? Would you bully a poor girl, just starting out her poker life?"

She thinks she is winning. I can see it in her face. She genuinely thinks that he is trying to get her to throw away her hand.

"Well, I really am not bluffing, so I am going to go all in," she says.

She moves her hands and counts her chips out one at a time into the middle of the table. "– forty, fifty, and sixty. Sixty dollars, all in."

She has dropped the 'pretend' now. This has suddenly become very real.

Her cheeks have started to fill with the red blush of excitement. She turns around to me and makes a little thumbs up gesture. I don't imagine this is a particularly good way to play poker, but she looks so happy right now.

Luke sees it too, that glow in her cheeks and the sparkle in her eyes. He slowly looks at his cards again, first one, and then the other, and finally looks back at Zoe, still facing me. I see a smile cross his face as he watches her. He runs one hand through his hair and taps the forefinger of his other on his cards.

"I have a big hand here, Zo," he says.

"Me too," she says. Her voice trembles slightly, but still I believe that it is the excitement of winning rather than the fear of being beaten. "You should fold. I'm winning this one. You don't want to get lucky and make me sad, do you?

Luke leans back in his chair. "Well, that wouldn't be fair at all, would it?" He looks at his cards one last time and says, "You've got me this time. Well played."

He slides his cards into the pile of discards and pushes his chips towards Zoe.

She lets out an excited squeaking noise and flips over her two cards. "Jacks!" she squeals. "Told you I had it."

Luke nods, smiles, and gathers the cards for the next hand.

When the game is over, the guys have gone home, and the three of us are cleaning up, I think about whether I should tell Zoe about what happened. Part of me wants to let her know that Luke did something sweet for her, but then again, she is so happy about having won a few hands that I don't want to burst her bubble. Maybe it means nothing. Maybe he was just being kind. I decide to bite my tongue, for now, and let her enjoy the evening for what it was.

Chapter Nine

Monday, week seven, first term. The time has finally come. Before I settled down for an early night, I set four separate alarms to make sure I didn't oversleep, but I still wake up before any of them sound. No lying in bed, scrolling through my phone this morning. I jump up and head straight down to the shower.

All I can think about while I am washing my hair, running the scrunchie over my body and scrubbing my face is that today I will get to put on my uniform for real. Today it's not just about being in the skills lab with my course mates. Today I will finally meet patients. My mentor, Stacey, is picking me up and taking me out on her day of visits. Today, tomorrow, the rest of the week, five days a week until Christmas break. No more classes, just this: practicing to be a midwife.

I hear the beeping of a car horn outside and look in the mirror one last time before I head out of the house. My first day on placement. My first day meeting pregnant women, postnatal women, and whatever else comes our way.

Zoe is in the kitchen, and she runs into the hallway to meet me before I leave.

"I'm so excited for you," she says. "I wish I could start my placements too."

"Not long, Zo," I smile.

We share a hug and then she makes a show of wiping her hand over my uniform, straightening me out.

The car horn beeps again.

"I'd better go! See you tonight."

"Have an awesome day," she says. She stands in the hallway as I leave.

I dash to the door, and out onto the pavement. Stacey is sitting in a smart looking blue car, writing in a thick book that's propped precariously on her steering wheel.

I tap gently on the window. She leans across the passenger seat, pushes the door open, and calls out to me.

"Violet? Hi. Get in."

I drop my bag into the footwell and slide down into the seat.

"Hi," I reply, and smile through my nerves. "Sorry I was just coming downstairs."

"No worries," she says. "We have plenty of time."

Stacey is dressed in the standard community midwife uniform of navy polo shirt and matching trousers. I was expecting a middle-aged woman, but the driver can't be any older than thirty. She's got long blonde hair, pulled back into a tidy ponytail, and she lifts her glasses up onto her head as she puts her diary away.

"Alright? Nervous?"

I nod and grin. "Looking forward to it though."

"We have a visit to go to, then we can stop off in the office, look at your paperwork and have a chat before we really get going." She smiles and puts me completely at ease.

I buckle my seatbelt over my grey shirt, and we set off towards the beginning of my first placement.

When we pull up at the side of the road, I feel the butterflies in my stomach begin the flutter. Part nervousness, part excitement, I fiddle with my hair, look into the mirror on the drop-down visor and try to focus.

"Hey," Stacey says. "This is a routine postnatal check. Nothing to worry about, I'll introduce you, and all you have to do is watch. Okay?"

I was hoping that my anxiety didn't show, but either I am completely transparent, or Stacey is really good at reading people.

"Thanks," I say quietly.

She pats me on the arm, reaches to pull her bag from the back seat and gets out of the car.

As I step onto the pavement, I hear her open and close the boot, and she hands me a large black bag to carry.

"Throw this over your shoulder," she says.

"Sure," I smile, happy to have a purpose.

I follow Stacey up the path to the front door of the house. The garden is small and tidy, and there are a pair of trendy potted olive trees, one to either side of the entrance. I have already started to form an impression of the family who must live inside, and I wonder how many times I will do this. Is it wrong to make a judgment before I even meet the woman, or should I be picking up information in a Sherlock-like way?

Stacey knocks, and a voice from within shouts, "Come in, it's open."

She pushes the door and we both walk into the house.

The hall leads straight into a smart living room with polished wooden floorboards and two chunky, deliciously comfortable looking beige sofas. There's a large mirror over a fireplace that houses a wood-burner. On one of the sofas, breastfeeding, is Sally Jeffries, the woman we have come to visit, the first mum I have met as a student midwife.

Stacey heads straight over to Sally and peers in at the feeding infant.

"You've got it cracked now," she says. "No more trouble?"

"It still hurts a little on the other side," Sally says, completely indifferent to the fact that a woman is staring at her exposed breast. "But I think that's because he wasn't latching properly there at first.

Much better now though, thanks."

"Good, good," Stacey says. She heads to the other sofa and sits down. Aware that I am still standing in the doorway, she beckons over to me. "This is Violet. It's her first day today."

"Hi, Violet. Do sit down. How's it going?"

Sally looks so comfortable feeding and chatting, it's hard to believe this is her first baby. She seems confident and in control.

"Good thanks. This is our first visit, so…I haven't had time to do anything wrong yet."

"Oh, bless you," Sally says. "I'm sure you won't do anything wrong. Stace will look after you. She's great."

"I pay her to say that," Stacey says.

She picks up Sally's notes from the table, and starts to write in them. I sit next to her and lean across, looking at what she is writing. Effortlessly, Stacey carries on chatting to Sally, making notes as she goes along. It doesn't even sound like she is running through the check boxes that are listed in the notes, but she is gathering all of the information that she needs to assess the baby's sleeping, feeding, bowel moments and micturition (or urination for the non-medical), checking on his general wellbeing.

"Are you getting enough rest?" she asks.

"I'm fine, yes. I have tried to sleep when Caleb sleeps, like you said. Takes a bit of getting used to, but I'm doing a lot better now." Without further prompting from Stacey, she says, "I've had a poo now too."

"Oh, great," Stacey says, and makes a mark in the notes. I suppose that this kind of conversation is my new normal. "How was it?"

I make an involuntary noise at this, and I have to apologise. "I'm so sorry."

"Not used to the toilet talk yet," Stacey laughs, and Sally joins her.

"You soon will be," Sally smiles. Caleb has finished his feed, apparently, as Sally tucks her breast away and brings the baby over to us.

"Do you need to have a look at him?"

"I was going to weigh him today," Stacey says.

"Sure, I'll undress him. I was going to change him anyway."

Stacey nods to me to get the scales out of the big bag that I carried in. I pull them out of the case and skilfully drop them onto my foot. They aren't heavy, but I feel the heat bloom in my cheeks as I blush.

"You okay there?"

"Fine," I splutter, trying to sound fine.

"Better not let you get your hands on Caleb just yet," Stacey says. I am mortified, but Sally laughs again, and I relax a little.

"Sorry!" I step back and let Stacey continue. She lays a soft blanket onto the scales and sets them to zero before laying the naked baby onto them. I would probably have put him straight onto the cold plastic and made him scream. There seems to be so much that I have to learn.

"Great, he's started to put on weight already," Stacey says. "A lot of babies, especially breastfed babies, can lose weight in the first few days. He is already up on his birthweight."

"That's brilliant," I add, trying to think of something helpful to say. I don't want Sally to think of me as just the ditsy student who can't do anything right.

Sally smiles proudly and starts to dress Caleb again. Nappy, Babygro, blanket, and then into the Moses basket at the end of the sofa. He doesn't make any kind of fuss, and I reflect that he is probably setting an unfairly high standard for all the future babies I will meet.

"Do you mind if I check your tum?" Stacey asks.

Sally lies on the sofa, and folds down the top of her trousers in a way that makes it clear she has done this many times before.

Stacey nods for me to join her and I stand by her side.

"I'm feeling for the top of the uterus, to make sure it is going back down as it should be doing."

I nod and smile at Sally. She doesn't seem to mind me looking at her, and she smiles back.

"Do you mind if Violet feels?" Stacey asks.

"Of course, no problem. I think I am fairly safe here," she laughs,

I smile and nervously edge to her side.

"So, start just below the umbilicus there, with your hand like I had mine. You'll need to press in a little, gently, but firmly. Okay, now, move down slightly towards the top of the pubis."

I follow her instructions carefully, fearful that I am going to use too much force, and hurt Sally in some way. At first, I feel only the gentle flab of the postnatal abdomen, completely normal, and then I reach the top of the uterus. I smile as I palpate it. I have practiced this on mannequins in the skills lab, and now here I am, on my placement, doing this for real.

"Here," I say to Stacey. "I can feel it."

Sally smiles at the excitement in my voice. "Bless you," she says. "You're going to make a great midwife; I can already tell."

My smile broadens, and Stacey rests her hand onto my shoulder.

"Good job, Violet. I think Sally might be right there."

By the time Stacey drops me off at home we have made two more postnatal visits, eaten a remarkably good meat and potato pie each from a little bakery she knows behind the clinic, gone through my paperwork, and carried out two antenatal booking appointments with women in early pregnancy. It's been a whirlwind of a day, and I'm happy to get into the living room and flop onto the sofa. It's gone four o'clock, but it seems I am the only one in the house. I make tea, turn on the television, and promptly fall asleep.

When I wake up an hour later, I see that I have been covered up in a thick brown fleece blanket, and my cold tea has been taken away. My mouth is dry, and my neck is sore from lying in an awkward position, but at least I am warm and cosy.

"Zoe?" I shout. There's no answer, so I rub my eyes, stretch, and get to my feet.

There's no sign of her downstairs, and she's not in her room or the bathroom on our floor either.

"Zoe?" I call again. Nothing.

"She's popped to the shop," a voice calls down from the top floor.

"Oh. Okay. Thanks." I look at the blanket that I have carried up. "Uh, thanks for this."

"No worries." I hear his feet hit the floor above and he comes down the stairs to meet me. "You feel okay? How was your first day in placement?"

I am about to answer when I hear the front door open.

"I guess she's home," Luke says

"It was great," I smile. "I'm knackered though."

He gestures towards the staircase and we head down to meet Zo.

She greets me with a massive hug.

"So?"

"It was fine," I say, trying to keep my face straight.

"Yeah, nothing special, I guess," she says. "Same as any other old day."

"Totally. I don't know what all the fuss was about."

"Uniform looks pretty sweet though."

"I met an adorable baby, and some great women too. My community mentor is just amazing. Oh, she's so cool…" I can't keep up the play façade any longer, I have to gush about the day I have had.

Zoe sits attentively, listening to every word, nodding in all the right places, and listening to everything I have to say. Luke has given up and headed into the kitchen. He's turning out to be an absolute sweetheart, but that doesn't mean he has to listen to the ins and outs of my day spent cooing over babies. Zoe, on the other hand, is stuck with me.

We have fallen into a routine at Tangiers Court. I'm still on day shift hours until next term, and the others are around most evenings. Zoe has managed to go to a few of the yoga classes that she signed up for, and Luke hangs out with his three friends sometimes, but apart from that we have fallen together as a group.

We take turns in making dinner – unless it's Andrew's turn, and then we have takeout. We have a rota for cleaning, and we work well as a team. Zoe and I have always been a dynamic duo; it's always been just the two of us. I never thought that anyone else would fit into our mini-team, but somehow Luke manages to fill a gap that we didn't even know was present.

Chapter Ten

My community placement flies by. Before I know it, it's mid-December. I'd like to be looking forward to the end of term. I love Christmas, what with all the sparkling lights and mulled wine. I also adore being able to shop for other people; it's the most amazing kind of guilt-free shopping. That's especially true when I'm shopping for Zo, because I am pretty much buying things that I like too.

I can't relax and get excited about it yet though. I will have a three week break after the end of my community placement, before the beginning of the next trimester, but first I have to hand in two assignments. I've been so caught up in placements that have hardly thought about my coursework.

I haven't been onto campus while I've been on placement, it seems strange to think that I was there for all of those weeks at the start of term. Not being on campus also means that I have been nowhere near the library. I've got a copy of 'Myles Textbook for Midwives' and 'Fundamentals of Midwifery' but that's as far as my textbook collection runs. There's a huge selection of texts on the university's online catalogue, apparently, but I haven't gotten near to starting yet. I'm going to have to put some work in if I want to get these papers finished and handed in on time.

I'm sitting at my desk, laptop open, mug of tea and two chocolate digestives to my side. I'm ready to get stuck into it.

That's when Zoe comes to my door.

"Hey," she says, in a voice that is not quite her usual tone.

"Come in," I say, nodding towards the bed, for her to sit down. "You alright?"

She nods and sits. "Sorry, were you…?"

"I haven't started yet. I was about to actually read my essay questions."

"Tell me about it. I have some waffle about pedagogy to write by the twentieth."

"Peda- what?" My brain runs a quick calculation. "Something about children?"

"Kind of." She seems restless. I get the feeling that she isn't here to talk about her essays.

"We can work together on them later if you like?"

"Study buddies!" She smiles, but there's something going on beneath. I wait a beat, to see if she wants to start talking or if I need to ask. She opens her mouth, and then stops. On the second attempt, she speaks. "I need some advice."

I get up and turn my chair around properly, so that I am looking at her face on.

"It's Luke," she says.

"What about him?"

"Do you think it would be a terrible thing to, you

know, try to start something with him? I mean we all live together, and I don't want things to be awkward for you, if we are, I mean if…well, you know what I mean."

"Oh," I say, without thinking. "Luke?" I pause to consider this, all the time watching Zoe, taking in her expression. She looks nervous, like a girl asking her father if she can date the boy next door. "You don't have to ask me, you know. If you like him, then of course you should go for it. We will be fine. I mean all of us, here; it will be fine."

"Vi, I know I don't need your permission. I…I suppose I was just…oh, I don't know."

"But you do know that you and I are always going to be there for each other, no matter what. We've dated people before; it never came between our friendship."

"I was worried more because, you know, now we live together, I don't want it to be all up in your face and…"

"Is this because I am not showing an interest in dating anybody? Do you feel bad that you have someone you like and I'm on my own?"

She breaks eye contact. "I guess, a little bit," she says.

"You don't have to worry about me. I told you from the start, I'm not here to meet someone. I want to pass my assignments." I gesture at my laptop. "I want to be a midwife. Anything else is a bonus. Or an interruption, depending on how it goes."

She doesn't say anything.

"Look, if it makes you feel any better, I will start dating Andrew. He's just my type anyway."

This raises a small laugh from Zoe. "He is very quiet."

"Strong silent type. Perfect. Won't make too many demands on my time…"

"I can't see him taking you anywhere exciting for a date though."

"Well, we enjoy our own space."

We both laugh, and it feels good. Seeing Zoe glow with excitement like this makes me feel a warm thrill inside too.

"I like how you just assumed he will be interested in me," she says.

"Who wouldn't be? You're the best. Beautiful, clever, funny…actually I'm surprised Andrew hasn't snapped you up already," I say. Again, I think about mentioning poker night, and how Luke let her win, but again I decide against it. I can be supportive without taking that victory away from her.

"Andrew never does his share of the housework," she smiles. "Thanks Vi. Same back at you. How about I make us both a brew and we can start on these assignments?"

"Sounds like a plan. And Zoe…of course he likes

you. I've seen the two of you. You have fun together. It will be amazing, I'm sure."

She gets up and flings her arms around me, giving me a firm, swift hug. "Thanks Vi. Good luck with Andrew." She winks and runs downstairs.

The rest of the evening is split between poring over the finer points of our essay writing, trying to work out how the Harvard referencing system works and how Zoe should approach Luke. That's seemingly easier than deciding whether we can use what someone said on Twitter as a valid argument in our essays, if we add the link to the tweet in the reference list.

We have a week left of term, which means a week left of my placement, a week to hand in this assignment and a week before Luke goes home for Christmas break.

"The way I see it, you can do this one of two ways," I say, my mind still half-thinking in academic arguments. "Some would argue that the most effective method would be to directly approach Luke and express your desire to…" I look at Zoe. "I was going to say date him. I assume you do want to date him, not just the, er…"

She digs me gently in the ribs, raises her finger to her lips in a 'shush' symbol and giggles.

"Okay, express your desire to bang him and date

him. Others may use the seasonal festivities as an opportunity to fabricate a conducive environment where alcohol, music and the Christmas spirit could influence the outcome of events…"

"What does the great scientist Violet Cobham think?" Zoe says, her voice as serious as she can make it through her laughter.

"Much as I think that getting drunk and festive is a great idea, I also believe that asking him when he is sober would be a better plan if you want more than just the banging. Imagine you have a drunken romp and then neither of you know where you stand; then it does all get kind of awkward around here."

"I think you're right." She taps a few final words onto her laptop and sits back. "You know, I've never been interested in one-night things. I don't want him to think that's all I want now."

"Talk to him. You have all week."

"All week. Sure." She smiles and mimes biting her nails in a faux-terrified movement.

"We managed to get our essays written. I feel like we can achieve anything," I say.

"I'll reserve judgement until I get my grades back," she replies, "and until I find the guts to ask him."

With the last of my coursework out of the way, I settle into enjoying the final week of my community placement. Between that first day, stepping out of the house in my uniform, and now has already felt like an incredible journey. It's only been four weeks, and I have a long way left to go.

I have started to fill in some of my PAD, and today Deb, my personal tutor from university, is coming out to meet Stacey and me after clinic to see how I have been getting on. We have our regular visits in the morning, three postnatals and an antenatal blood pressure check, and then it's back to the office for lunch.

Stacey is trying to chat to me about my plans for Christmas, but all I can think about is the impending meeting with Deb.

"We always go to his mother's of course, what with her being…" She pauses midsentence, mug in one hand, sandwich in the other. "Are you alright, Violet?"

I haven't touched my lunch. Stacey knows me well enough by now for this to concern her. I'm usually the first to put the kettle on, make tea, get my food out and tuck in.

"Mmm," I say. "It's nothing. I'm fine."

"When people say that something is nothing, it is still a something. What's up?"

My stomach is turning over, and I'm afraid that if I eat my packed lunch, I will be bringing up the cheese salad. I don't feel hungry at all. Quite the opposite.

"Just a little nervous about the meeting," I say. "I'm being silly, I know."

"Nothing to worry about," Stacey smiles. "You have been great on this placement. Deb coming to see me is a formality. It's what they do. They like to check that you are okay, and that we are okay supporting you. Alright? Nothing to be scared of."

I nod slowly and try to believe. Logically, of course I know that it is the truth, but my niggling, doubting brain still wants to have me believe that my tutor is coming to tell me that I am not good enough.

I nibble at my sandwich and raise it to show Stacey. She smiles again.

"Honestly, it's all fine. You do worry."

I do. I always do.

Deb Cross arrives bang on time at 12:45 and we leave the break room for the privacy of the consultation room. I feel like I am being interviewed all over again. The room feels smaller than it usually does when we are working in here, and it's making me claustrophobic. There's only one small window, and it doesn't let in enough light or air. Why have I never noticed this before? How could I have expected women to sit in this room and discuss their pregnancies with me when I can't bear to be in here myself? The thought makes the nausea throb harder within me.

"Such a lovely clinic," my link tutor says. "How have you been getting on? Do you like community?"

Stacey looks at me supportively. My hands are starting to feel clammy, so I slide them beneath my thighs and semi-sit on them.

"Yes," I say. My voice comes out like a shaky squeak. I clear my throat. "I've been really enjoying it."

I can almost hear Stacey's thoughts, willing me to have the confidence to keep talking. I can feel the warmth radiate from her.

"It feels like I have been out here for months, not weeks." I stop, and then I add quickly, "But I know I have so much to learn." I don't want to say the wrong thing. I don't want Deb to think I am cocky or overconfident. That is probably even worse than a lack of confidence.

"That's good." Deb writes some notes in her file. "What kind of things have you been doing?"

"Do you need to see my PAD?" I hand it over. "I've started to get some of my competencies signed off. It's been a mixture really. Antenatal, postnatal, and baby checks."

The tutor skim reads the contents of my document. "Great. You've seen a lot already, that's super." She turns to Stacey. "Sounds like it has been a good learning experience?"

"Violet is so good with the women and their families. She's a natural."

I feel my cheeks flush red, and I look away. I don't know if I find it difficult to hear positive things about myself because I don't believe them, or if it is just a natural response to feel this way.

"I'll miss having her with me."

I'll miss being with Stacey too.

"Will I come back here on my next community placement?" I ask.

"We do try to keep students out in the same areas, yes. As long as Stacey is able to take you, you'll come back here. It probably won't be until either the end of this academic year or into next year though." She runs a finger down the page in her planner. "You'll have postnatal or antenatal next, and then the delivery unit."

"Postnatal next," I say. "I got the email through."

She nods and makes a note. "You know before I do," she smiles. "So, yes. Chances are you'll be back."

"I'll look forward to it," Stacey says, and I know how much I will too.

Every placement is going to be full of new experiences and learning opportunities, but this has been special. I love being out on the road, visiting women in their own homes, helping out in the clinics. I could see myself choosing to work in community after I qualify. That's a long time away.

When I get back to Tangiers Court, Zoe is already home, sitting at the kitchen table, chatting to Luke.
"How was it?" she asks.
I pull the biscuit jar out of the cupboard and take a bite out of a Jammie Dodger.
"Yurmh," I say. I swallow and repeat myself. "Yeah. It was fine. Unsurprisingly I was stressing about nothing."
"The great triumvirate?" Luke says. "It sounds like an ancient Roman firing squad."

"I'm not sure the ancient Romans had guns, Luke," Zoe laughs, leaning in towards him.

"You can have a firing squad with, uh…" He pauses, racking his brain. "Tridents? What the heck did Romans use?"

"Who knows?" I say. "Whatever. It was fine anyway. And it's tripartite," I say. That's what the university calls it when the three of us meet to discuss my placement. Link tutor, placement mentor and student: three parts.

I eat the rest of the biscuit in two bites and hover at the edge of the table, looking at them. "So…"

Zoe shakes her head in a subtle move that Luke doesn't catch.

"Right," I say. "Okay."

He gives me a look, and I try to think of a new

subject. "What's for dinner?"

"Andrew's turn," Zoe smiles.

"I wonder if he will show up after the holidays?" Luke says. "It would be nice to have another man around the house."

"Hey! What's wrong with us?" Zoe says in mock indignation.

"I'm surprised you even have to ask." He says it with a deadpan tone that can only be interpreted as a joke.

Zoe feigns offence, turning her back and raising her nose into the air. I hope she gets on with asking him soon. The tension is enough to make me want to push them together. It also makes me feel something that I haven't felt for some time. Ever since my last relationship I have been quite happy to be on my own and single. I mean, I'm only eighteen still. It's not like I have been on my own for years, falling into a pit of spinsterhood. Seeing Zoe, the way she is around Luke, and now that I think about it, the way he is around her, it makes me…well, it makes me think that maybe I would like someone like that in my life too. I can barely keep up with coursework, placements, and day to day existence, but I could possibly find space in my life for the right person. Who knows?

Zoe is scrolling through takeaway options on her phone. "Pizza? Indian? What do you guys fancy?"

"We only have a few days left here. Do you fancy going out to eat tonight?"

This could be an opportunity for Zoe. I open my mouth into an exaggerated yawn and stretch my arms above my head. I never was all that good at drama, but I am doing my best. "You two go, I think I'm going to shove something in the microwave and have an early night."

"Not much point just the two of us going out," he says, and looks over Zoe's shoulder at the food options. "Let's order pizza?"

"I quite fancy it now Violet's mentioned it," Zoe says. I know she is probably trying to sound cool and act naturally, but I can hear the flirtation in her voice. I almost smile and nudge her, but I hold it back.

"You should go. Really. Don't worry about me. You know what I'm like. It's been a tough few weeks. I fancy a bath and some chicken ding."

Chicken ding is what we have come to call any ready meal that consists at least in part of chicken and is reheated in the microwave. Ding! It's ready.

There's a slight pause, and then Zoe and Luke both start to speak at once. She begins with "it doesn't matter if.." and he is about to say "we can go…" but both of them get tangled up at once and there's an awkward exchange while they try to decide who should say their words first. I'm not sure if the tension between them is so obvious to me because Zoe has told me how she feels, or if it is just blatantly evident. Luke must be able to tell what she is feeling, surely?

I rub my temples melodramatically. "I'm starting to get a headache," I say. "You two go ahead. I'm going to run the bath and chill."

"Let me get you some paracetamol," Luke says. He leaps over to the cupboard, and Zoe flashes me a sharp, nervous glance.

"This is it!" I mouth, making sure I don't say anything loudly enough for Luke to hear.

She makes a silent movement, gripping her fists together, and miming a squeal of excitement and I let out a tiny laugh.

"You okay?" Luke hands me two small round tablets and a half glass of water.

"Thanks, er yeah. I'll…" I stop myself from talking before I end up saying something stupid.

I make my way upstairs, alone. I don't really have a headache at all, so I drop the painkillers onto my table and knock back the water. It's going to be a long night.

I sit alone in my room, flick through social media for a while and then pick up the book I have been slowly reading. I was doing the right thing for Zoe by faking the headache and coming up here, but I should probably have thought about bringing some food with me. I read about three pages before I hear someone coming up the stairs.

"We're getting pizza after all," she says. Her eyes tell me everything I need to know about how she is feeling.

"Oh, I'm sorry, Zo. I thought that if I got out of the way you might have some time alone together, maybe go out…"

"I know and thank you. Thanks for doing that, but once you came up here, I don't know, it was like he didn't want to talk anymore."

"Ugh. Really, I'm sorry. I don't know what to say."

"You might as well come down. We'll get some food, and," she shrugs, "enjoy our last few days of term, I suppose."

"And what are you going to do about Luke?"

"Hope the right time presents itself. Flirt a little. Be my usual wonderful self until he falls desperately in love with me."

We both laugh. Why wouldn't he fall for her? Zoe is the best.

Before I know it, it's Friday. The end of the first trimester has come around more quickly than I could have imagined. Last day of term, last day of placement; for me, and for Zoe too.

At breakfast she prods at her toast and sips at the coffee that she usually guzzles down. There are only twenty minutes left before Stacey will arrive to take me to our last visits of the term, but I hate leaving Zoe like this.

"Want to talk about it?" I ask.

She shrugs and breaks a piece off her toast. Instead of eating it, she tears another piece, and then another. All her concentration is centred on creating a pile of cubed, crumby bread on her plate. More accurately, all her concentration is elsewhere, and desiccating her breakfast is what she is absent-mindedly doing instead of focusing on eating.

"Shall I make you something else?"

She shakes her head, without looking at me.

"Okay. Well." It's one of those moments when I know that she has so much that she wants to say, but she doesn't know where to start. I've seen this before. I know her mind must be filled with so many issues.

"Holidays? Uni? Luke? All of the above?"

This time, she nods, picks up one of the decimated pieces of her breakfast and sticks it into her mouth.

"Oh Zo. I'm sad that term is ending too. We have so much more to do after the holidays though. Do you not want to get home, have Christmas, see your folks?"

"Of course," she mutters, almost too quietly for

me to hear.

"There's still tonight if you want to, you know, talk to Luke."

This provokes a heaving sigh.

"It's too late now. I don't want to start something up on the last day. I don't think I could bear to get close to him now and have to leave for three weeks. Better to wait and…" She trails off. "I don't know. Not now though. I left it too late."

"He'll be back in January, just like us." I stop sharply, as Luke's footsteps thunk down the stairs. Zoe rolls her eyes and starts to chain-eat the rest of her toast.

Luke looks over her shoulder as he passes towards the cupboard. "Morning," he says in a voice that sounds much more awake than he appears.

"Hey," I say. Zoe waves her hand in a greeting gesture, her mouth full.

"Last day, eh? I finish at lunchtime. Probably going to set off for home this afternoon," Luke says.

Crumbs fly out onto the table as Zoe coughs out her toast.

"This afternoon?"

"Yeah, some of the gang back home want to go out tonight to celebrate. Pre-Christmas thing, you know. Don't want to miss that. Hey, are you alright?"

Zoe is still coughing, so I pass her my water, and

nod at her to drink.

"Should I slap you on the back?" Her face is deep red, but she raises a hand to me, and inhales deeply.

"I'm fine," she says, still breathless. "Fine."

"I have to go in a few minutes, Luke. We didn't even get to say goodbye properly," I say.

"I would have thought you two would be sick of the sight of my ugly mug by now, ladies." He puts his bowl of cereal on the table and sits between us, thrusting his spoon into what appears to be a mixture of chocolate crispies and corn flakes. "Couldn't decide which to have," he says, by way of explanation.

There's the beeping of a car horn form outside. All I can do is give Zoe a helpless look.

"Well, that's me. Uh, have a great Christmas then, Luke and we'll see you next year."

"If I come back," he says, with a wicked smile.

From the look on Zoe's face, I think she is close to coughing her toast up again, but she manages to hold it together. "I'd better leave too," she says. It's earlier than she needs to set off, but I guess she doesn't want to be here with Luke this morning. Not like this.

When I stand up, Luke reaches out to give me a hug. "Happy Christmas, Vi."

I pat him gently on the back. "Thanks, mate."

Zoe scuttles to her feet too and reaches out to him

expectantly, and possibly a little too eagerly. He grabs hold of her and lifts her slightly off the floor as he squeezes her tightly. She's about a foot shorter than he is, so it's quite easy for him to swing her up.

I can't see her face, because it's buried into his chest, but I know that her expression will be somewhere between agony and ecstasy. I wait for him to release her, and when she turns away to walk to the door with me, she looks close to tears. I link arms with her and pull her close to me.

"Plenty of time," I say quietly, "Plenty of time."

And that is how we end the term. I finish my final day in my placement, Zoe has her last classes, and when we return to the house, Luke has gone.

Chapter Eleven

If the weeks at university passed more quickly than I expected, the Christmas holidays feel like months rather than weeks. Despite being my favourite time of the year, before we even get to Christmas Day, I am itching to get back to Tangiers Court, to lectures, and to my next placement. My agitation is nothing compared to Zoe's though. All that stuff about absence making the heart grow fonder is working for her. I can't help but wonder if it is having the same effect on Luke too. Apart from a few texts on Christmas Day though, neither of us hear from him.

On the first weekend of the new year, we bundle our bags into Zoe's Corsa and make our way back to uni.

Classes start again on Monday, and I am more than ready to get stuck in. This term we have three weeks of lectures and then I am rostered for my first rotation onto the postnatal ward. I had hoped that I would get the delivery suite as my next placement, but I won't have my slot there until April. Those four months seem a long way into the future. I have to assist in the delivery of forty babies while I am a student. I'll probably have finished my first year before I even get to see a baby being born.

I'm prepared for the start of term, everything laid out ready for the morning. Zoe and I have decided to have a chill night and binge watch Netflix rather than going onto campus for the Returners' Party in the SU bar.

It's Sunday evening, gone seven o'clock, and there is still no sign of Luke. It feels strangely quiet with just the two of us. Although we have been best friends since we met as toddling three-year olds, and even silence between us has never felt completely empty, it feels like there is something missing. I hadn't realised quite how much a part of our lives Luke has become until now. I'm sure Zoe must be feeling that even more acutely than I.

"He is coming back, isn't he?" Her face bears a deadly serious expression.

"Of course," I say. "He was laughing when he told us he wasn't coming back." He must have been joking, surely. "And he would have said something when he texted, wouldn't he?"

She nods and reaches out for the cushion on the sofa next to her, pulling it in front of her and cradling it in her arms like a hug.

"You could message him?" I suggest.

She buries her face into the cushion.

"Or I could?" I say the words even though I don't really want to be the one to message him. I will do it for Zoe if it is going to make her feel better. He is coming back though; he must be.

"No!" She almost shrieks the word. "Don't. He'll

be back."

I smile. "And when he is? What are your plans?"

"My plan is that he will tell me how much he has missed me while he was away and declare his undying love for me." She waves her arms out in a melodramatic gesture and I can't help laughing.

"That sounds like an excellent plan."

Despite three weeks of lie-ins and lazy days over the holidays, I am up as soon as my first alarm sounds on Monday morning, and I'm out of the door with Zoe bang on time.

At nine o'clock, the hubbub in the lecture room is drawn to a sharp cessation by the arrival of our module leader. New term, new lecturer.

"Nice to see you all back and ready to learn," she says.

The lecturer is a tall, stern-looking brunette. Her hair is short-bobbed, and its sharpness emphasises her dark eyes and prominent cheekbones. She must be close on six feet tall, even in the ballet pumps she's wearing with her no-nonsense pencil skirt and blouse. It is almost as though she is the polar opposite of Zita. I gently nudge Sophie and raise my eyebrows.

"Seems strict," I mouth, and she nods subtly in collusion.

"Now you are all settled into the course, we are

going to start on this year's real work. Last term you all had FUN?" She says it as though it is an accusation, and throughout the class students turn to each other creating a susurration of whispers. The lecturer picks up the dry wipe marker. "This term we are going to be having…"

I expect her to utter something terrifying, but instead she says, "FUN too!"

She writes FUN2 in bold, curvy letters on the centre of the board.

"I know. They could have thought of a more creative name for it." She smiles, and it is as though we all let out a collective breath that we were holding.

"Welcome to Fundamentals of Midwifery Two!"

She pulls out the sign-in sheet and passes it to one of the girls at the front of the class to circulate.

"I'm Rachel Rogers, and I will be your tutor throughout this module."

I settle into my chair, pick up my pen, and focus. I get the feeling that this is going to be a great class.

"Before we make a start, have you all had a chance to read through the module guide?"

Most of my classmates mumble variations of 'yes', and I nod along.

"Good. Then you will know that this term you will have your first OSCE." She pronounces it 'oss-kee', but my mind flits to the name, 'Oscar', and I can't help but think about a glitzy award ceremony.

From the sighed groans throughout the room, it's evident that the OSCE this term is not going to be glamourous in the slightest.

"OSCE," she repeats. "The Objective Structured Clinical Examination. Basically, it's a role play, but a role play that you are going to be assessed on. This is, as the name suggests, an exam. You need to pass this exam to continue with your course."

Suddenly this feels less like FUN and more along the lines of the terror that I had first imagined. I had heard of the OSCE before we got to class, but my trepidation about the examination hadn't struck me until she said its name out loud. It's almost as though it didn't feel real when it was only letters that I had read on a screen. Rachel has conjured up the OSCE monster, and now it is looming in the not-too-distant future.

Rachel is still talking. "An actress plays the role of the patient, and the student, which will be you, will work through a scenario, making clinical decisions and behaving exactly as they would in a real-life situation."

The room has fallen into a stunned silence. Rachel clicks her heels over to the computer. "The first year OSCE is meant to be the easiest," she says.

My hands are clammy even at the thought of the assessment. It sounds like my idea of hell. I thought that presentations were my worst nightmare, but this is a new low. I've never had to do anything like this before but being critically observed while I am trying to act naturally, professionally, and safely fills me with a stomach clenching dread. I have three months to get it together.

"You will prepare for six scenarios. We are going to work through them in class, and they will be experiences that you are likely to encounter in your practice placements. There is nothing to be afraid of. This is basic midwifery care." She sounds so matter of fact.

I look at the letters that I have written onto my notepad, 'FUN2', and I scribble them out, obliterating them in a cyclone of black ink.

When I get back to Tangiers Court, I find Zoe, sitting on her bed, with her knees hugged up to her chest. She's got her headphones on, and hasn't heard me coming up the stairs, so she jumps a little as I peek around the door into her room.

"What's up?"

"Just chilling," she says, but the words are flat and empty.

"Have you eaten? Do you want a drink or anything?"

She shrugs and puts her headphones down on the bedside table. Our rooms are essentially the same, just laid out differently. The head of her bed faces towards the window, so she can sit exactly as she is now, and look out into the garden. I wonder how long she has been here, huddled up, doing just that.

"I'm fine," she says. "Really, I'm okay."

I perch on the edge of her bed.

"He's not back?"

She shakes her head.

"His stuff is still here," she says, nodding her head towards the door and the stairs up to the top floor. "So, he must be coming back."

"Unless he doesn't care about his stuff. Or unless something has -" I stop myself from completing the sentence. I don't want to think anything bad has happened, and I definitely don't want Zoe to think it.

Zoe finishes my thought anyway. "Happened to him?" She pulls herself into a more upright sitting position, flattening her legs out on the bed. "Do you think…? Has something…?" She frowns. "No. No."

"Hey, I'm sure that he is fine." I put my hand onto her ankle, making contact, trying to calm her. "He probably had something to deal with at home. He loves his course almost as much as we love ours. He's never given any indication that he doesn't want to be here."

"Leeds is a long way away. If something has happened maybe he can't get back here to get his stuff. Or perhaps it's down to someone else to come and collect it and they have other priorities." She takes a big gulp of air. I can hear that her breathing has become faster, and she is trying to get a hold of herself. "He never messaged over the holidays -"

"He sent us both a text on Christmas Day," I remind her. She waves the comment away.

"Apart from that. I mean, he didn't exactly keep in touch. I thought he would be back over the weekend, but the first day of term is over and he's still not here. He can't love his course that much."

I don't know what to tell her. A part of me is equally as confused as she is. Then again, how well do we know him? We have shared a house for three months, sure, but how long does it take to really get to know somebody?

"I'll message him," I say. It's the obvious thing to do. I'll check if he is alright. Zoe perks up at the suggestion.

"I was going to," she says, "but I don't want to come across as…well, you know."

I nod and smile. "I know. And it's fine for me to message because I don't want to…"

She tilts her head, raises her eyebrows and I don't have to finish my sentence. We both know what she wants to do with him.

My phone is in the bottom of my bag. I take it out and tap in a simple message:

Thought you'd be back by now. You okay?

I turn the screen to Zoe, and ask for her approval.

"Do you think that sounds like we are checking up on him? Should we change it to something less, I don't know, accusative?" she says.

"You think it sounds accusative?

"Maybe. A little." She smiles a tiny smile, trying to keep light-hearted.

"I don't know how to ask without it sounding like that," I say. I delete what I have written and type:

When are you coming back?

That sounds worse, so I delete it immediately, and stare at my screen, hoping for inspiration to strike. Finally, I grin at Zoe and enter:

Andrew is asking to swap rooms with you. Should we let him?

Zoe gives that the thumbs up, and I send the message off into cyberspace, to Luke, wherever he is.

Zoe shuffles along the bed to sit next to me, and we both hunch over my phone, anticipating an instant reply. It doesn't come.

"Maybe he hasn't seen it yet, or he could be busy. Let's have dinner and see what happens?" I put my arm around her shoulder and give a little squeeze.

We cook, eat and clear away dinner. I want to talk to Zoe about the OSCE, but her mind is full of Luke, and I don't want to interrupt her with my worries.

He hasn't replied to my message, and I don't know what to make of it. Maybe he's not into texting. I mean, in all the time that we have been here, apart from the Happy Xmas texts, we have only exchanged messages when one or the other of us has wanted something from the supermarket.

We live together, and texting seems superfluous when we are in the same building most of the time, but perhaps it's just not something he does. Zoe and I, on the other hand, do text each other quite regularly, even when we are in the same room, never mind other parts of the house. Is it a girl thing, or a best friend thing? Are we both expecting too much of him if we expect a reply?

I'm starting to worry about him, so I can't imagine what Zoe must be thinking. One thing I do know - she must tell him how she feels.

Chapter Twelve

Despite not hearing back from Luke, when I drag myself, less than enthusiastically, out of bed on Tuesday morning, I run into him on the stairs. He's on his way up, I'm going down for breakfast.

"You scared me to death!" I yelp. It actually does sound like I am yapping at him, but I really didn't expect to see him here right now.

We stand on the staircase, which is the most cramped and ridiculously tight area to have a conversation.

"Sorry," he says, "I literally just got back."

I don't know what to say. My look must convey my disbelief, because he smiles and tries to give me an explanation.

"My lectures don't start until this morning, and I..." He stops before finishing the sentence, and when he talks again, I assume that he has changed what he was going to say. "I had some things to do back home."

"You've driven from Yorkshire overnight?"

He nods.

"Do you want to get past? I need a shower, then I'll come down and chat, if you have time."

I look at the clock on my phone screen.

"Sure."

I move to the side, and he heads up to his room.

I stand on the stairs briefly, trying to make sense of it. Something feels off, but I'm not sure what it is.

I turn and head back up to the landing.

"Zo?" I tap lightly on her door.

She takes a few moments to walk across her room and pop her head out. She only opens the door a crack; by the way she is gripping her duvet I can tell she isn't dressed yet.

"Was that Luke?" she asks. Although she's still half asleep, her excitement shows through in her voice.

I bob my head in a nod. "Yep. He's back."

"Why didn't he answer your message? Where has he been?" Her voice is a loud whisper, designed for me to hear and Luke not to.

I can only shrug. "Get dressed. He'll be down soon."

"Okay," she says, and ducks back into her room, pulling the door closed behind her.

By the time Luke comes downstairs, showered and dressed, Zoe and I are both at the kitchen table. She's hardly touched her breakfast.

"Alright?" he says, flopping into his usual chair, and plopping his bowl of chocolate crispies down.

"Where were you?" Zoe's tone is harsh and accusing. It's not really what I would have recommended if she is still trying to ingratiate herself with Luke.

"Woah!" He lifts his hands up in mock offence, at least I hope it's mock. "Sorry girls, I didn't mean to miss the sign-in." He says it with a smile and starts to tuck into his cereal.

I breathe a little relieved sigh and flash Zoe a look that's as sharp as her voice.

"Sorry," she says. "We didn't know where you were."

"Andrew was really worried," I add, trying to keep it light.

Luke angles his spoon upwards, pointing to where Andrew would be if he were in bed. And if he existed. "He wanted to muscle in on my room as soon as I was a day late back. I'm not sure I trust him anymore."

I pull a playful tight-lipped smile and give him a nudge that almost sends his crispies flying off his spoon.

Zoe seems to have been struck mute.

"So…where were you?" I ask, mimicking Zoe's tone, trying to turn it into a joke.

There's a moment of silence while Luke finishes his mouthful. Before he refills, he pauses, puts both hands palm down flat on the table and addresses us in a bold, serious voice. "I was with a girl."

The temperature in the room feels as though it drops five degrees in that moment. Zoe picks up her phone from the table, pretends to look at the time, and clatters to her feet, almost knocking her chair over.

"I've got to go," she says. She turns, nearly walking into the doorframe, and hurries out of the house.

"Is that the time? Gosh." I know that I am a terrible actress, but it's the best I can do under the circumstances. I scoop up my bag and chase after my best friend, leaving Luke looking at his bowl in bewilderment.

Chapter Thirteen

Five weeks into term, the mornings start to feel a little brighter. February brings the promise of coming spring. There are daffodils trying to sprout in the tiny front garden of Tangiers Court, little yellow buds on dancing stalks of green. It's warmer too. We have already started to discuss getting an outdoors table for the backyard so we can breakfast out there, and sit under the stars in the evenings when it's warm enough to enjoy it. When I say we, I mean Zoe and me. We are the ones poring over Pinterest, getting excited about pictures of cups of coffee on delicate white metal tables, but I assume that if we set it up, Luke will happily join us.

Information about Luke's female friend has been non-existent. Neither Zoe nor I want to ask for further details, but in our conversations about the mysterious woman we both speculate and secretly hope that he will reveal more about her of his own volition. Zoe reasons that if she asks too many questions, she will risk showing him her true feelings, and now they seem "a bit bloody pointless". I can't help but agree.

February also brings my first in-hospital placement. We are randomly allocated to antenatal, postnatal or delivery, and I am on my way to the Margaret

Beresford Unit – St. Jude's Hospital's postnatal ward. Despite this being another new environment to adjust to, I don't have the apprehension and anxiety before starting this placement that I did with my community visits.

I expected that I would; I thought that the night before I started, I would be sitting on my bed, filled with dread and self-doubt, but it didn't happen. Instead, I am heading to the afternoon shift, for my first day in the hospital, full of the joys of (coming) spring and unfaltering optimism.

My mentor for this placement is Geri Smith. All I know before I meet her is her name. I phoned up last week to find out what shifts she is, and by definition I am, working. As much as possible we are encouraged to work to the same shift pattern as our mentors. I've no reason not to work the same days, nights, and weekends as Geri. This shift pattern is going to be my future, I may as well start getting used to it.

The postnatal unit is an old-fashioned set-up. The midwifery office is at the centre, opposite the entry door, and the ward itself stretches off to the east and west. The arms of the unit are Nightingale style, beds separated only by curtain from neighbouring beds, and one central gangway.

Closer to the midwives' office are a cluster of side rooms, which are allocated to women who have the greatest need of them. That might be due to a prolonged stay due to maternal complications, infection requiring isolation of mother or baby, or a mother whose baby is on the neonatal intensive care unit. The side rooms have en suite bathrooms, and there are shared toilet and shower rooms for the other women on the ward to use.

To the direct left of the midwives' room is the Head of Midwifery's personal office. Next to that, the kitchen. It's for staff use only, as the women have their nutritious and not so delicious hospital meals delivered to them from the main hospital kitchens.

There's a storeroom, a medicines room, a linen room, and a sluice. Luckily, the sluice is far away from the bed spaces and from the midwives' office, because that's where the bedpans are emptied, and the rubbish is sent down the chute in colour-coded bags.

It's all very new to me. I've never been a hospital patient, apart from a quick visit to accident and emergency when I was in primary school. I was trying to give someone a piggy-back and fell and cracked my chin on a sharp desk corner. Seven stitches and a sugar-free lolly; that's my only experience of being a patient. I had never entered a ward until I walked onto the Margaret Beresford Unit.

After handover, Geri pulls a chair up next to where I am sitting in the midwives' office. She eyes me in the way a lion might look at an antelope. Not that I think she is going to eat me, but her gaze makes me shuffle uncertainly in my seat. I put my hands beneath my thighs to keep them from shaking.

"You've done postnatal checks in the community," Geri says: a statement, not a question. "A lot of what you will do as routine here is pretty much the same."

I smile and let out a relieved breath before she continues. She's to the point, but her voice is soft. I can feel my heart rate steadying itself.

"A lot of it will also be very different. We have women who have been transferred after Caesarean sections, so there is a lot of post-surgical care. You're not a nurse, are you?"

I shake my head. Some students have done their nurse training first, before converting to midwifery, but clearly, I have not.

"Hmm, okay," she says. I'm sure I can hear a trace of judgment in her voice, but I try to ignore it. I can do this just as well as anyone else at my level. I know I can. Still, her words do nothing to help my nervousness about the new placement.

I say nothing, and when she gets up and starts to walk, I follow Geri down the ward.

We are looking after four women and their

babies this morning. Two of the women have had Caesarean sections within the past week. One of the other women had a forceps delivery, and the final patient is a first-time mum who has been having some breastfeeding support.

Geri stops next to the first bed we come to.

"Morning, Fran," she says, smiling at the woman who is sitting up in the bed.

"Hi Geri," she replies.

"This is Violet, she is a student midwife working with me today. I'm going to get her to check you over, if that's okay?"

"Fine, no problem," Fran says. "Do you need my belly first?"

She's clearly used to the postnatal checks; she's lifting the sheet back to show me her Caesarean wound before I have time to even get to the bedside.

"Looks like it is healing well," I say, trying to sound professional. "Very clean."

I run through the rest of her check, but when it comes to reading her blood pressure, I pause. I've done this before, countless times, in the community, but always with a manual blood pressure monitor – a sphygmomanometer. Here, I am faced with a blue machine on a pole next to Fran's bed. Turning it on is easy; there's a button that says POWER. After pressing that, I stand and look at Geri.

"I haven't used one of these before," I say, hoping

that I don't come across as incompetent to Geri or to Fran.

"That's okay. Fasten the cuff around Fran's arm, like with a manual sphyg." I wrap the blue band around her arm and look at Geri again.

"Just press that button, and it will record the blood pressure and pulse," she says.

I'm sure I hear her sigh, but I concentrate on what I am doing, and try to shrug off the idea.

I push the button that she is pointing to, and the cuff starts to inflate. Fran sits, watching, as though this has become a natural part of her life now.

The machine beeps softly and flashes up a result, which looks fine.

"All good," I smile, take off the cuff and jot down the reading before I forget.

Geri doesn't smile, or at least she doesn't smile at me. Instead she gestures to the tube poking out from beneath Fran's sheets.

"Check the catheter," she says.

I look at her blankly. Check what? Check it's there? Check what it's doing? It doesn't look like it is doing anything. There's a bag at the end of the tube, and there is definitely urine in the bag, but that doesn't give me many clues as to what I am meant to be checking.

My uncertainty must show in my hesitance.

"Check the catheter, Violet," Geri says again.

"I don't know what I do," I say. "I haven't looked after anyone with a catheter before."

"This is why you students should be nurses before they train as midwives," Geri says, but she speaks to Fran rather than to me. She steps in front of me, practically pushing me out of the way. "Watch," she tells me.

I want to learn, and I want to watch, but my head swims in embarrassment - and the feeling that I am completely useless.

Fran doesn't seem to have picked up on my ineptitude. Her baby has started to stir, and her focus switches to the cot.

Geri completes the rest of the check herself. "You'd better just watch from now on," she says. "Until you start to learn."

I gulp and nod impotently. I am here to learn, that's true, but I am not sure that destroying my confidence is the best way for Geri to teach me.

It's an arduous shift. Even with only a few patients to care for, my placement mentor keeps me on my toes, and indeed on my feet, for the full seven and a half hours. At the end of the day, Geri stops me before I leave.

"Violet," Geri says. "You have a lot to learn, especially seeing as you have all of the basic nursing practice to catch up on, but I think we can get you through."

A tight ball catches in my throat. That was definitely a back-handed compliment.

"T-thanks."

"See you tomorrow afternoon," she says.

She walks away leaving me standing at the front of the maternity block, wondering exactly what to expect from this placement. I'm here for six weeks. I want to learn. I want to love this, but can I get through the next month and a half?

I catch the bus back from the hospital to Tangiers Court with tears in my eyes that I refuse to let fall. I won't be beaten. I have to push on; I have to show Geri that I can do this.

Chapter Fourteen

I spend the rest of the night up in my room. When Zoe knocks on my door, I don't even want to answer. I need some time.

"Hey," I shout, not getting up.

"You okay?" She stays outside the door. She must sense that something is wrong. I could count on one hand the number of times that I have closed my door since we have been here.

"Yeah," I say, but I am not convincing anybody, least of all myself.

"Shall I come back later?"

"Okay," I say, just loud enough to be heard.

Something about today has sapped me of all my energy. I've tried my hardest, done my best, but perhaps I lack the knowledge and skills that I need to succeed. Maybe I will never be able to be a midwife.

Zoe pauses outside my door for a little longer, even though I am silent. I know she is there. I listen for the sound of her feet moving away but hear nothing. She waits, and gradually I pull myself to my feet and head over to the door to let her in.

As soon as I see her, I can't hold back my emotions any longer. I reach out to hold her and collapse into a wave of throbbing sobs.

She says nothing, stroking my hair and holding

me close for what feels like an eternity, the two of us standing there on the tiny landing between our two rooms.

"Hey," she says, eventually. "It's alright, it's alright. Come on, let's sit down and you can tell me what happened."

I nod, and step back. My face is soggy, and I need to blow my nose. I tug a tissue out from the box by my bed before we both sit, and I tell her about my shift.

"She sounds awful," Zoe says. "What's wrong with her? Treating you like that. Awful."

"It could be me. The way I took it. I mean, on the surface, she didn't say anything wrong, but…"

"I think she meant it, from what you said. Don't make excuses for her."

I've been used to being told I am wrong, that I am not good enough, that I can't achieve anything. I have heard that from my father for so many years. I don't know why I thought that I could ever be a midwife, I don't know why I thought I could ever do this.

"Hey," Zoe says to my silence. "Stop thinking. Okay. Stop it."

We have been through this, or at least situations like this, before.

"I can't do it though. I can't, can I? I'll never be able to…"

"Stop it, Violet." She takes the tissue off me, and wipes at my eyes.

"Ugh!" I protest, but she wipes, and sets my face straight, then she pulls me upright.

"Come on. This isn't you. You're not that person anymore. You're not scared now. That's all behind you."

I thought it might be, I thought I could have left that behind, but it seems I was wrong. All the self-doubt I have ever felt has come back.

I don't know what to say to Zoe. I want to be strong. I want to be able to nod and agree and pick myself up and get it together and…I can't.

I let out a tearful sigh.

She tries a different tack.

"My placements have been tough too," she says. "I have to stand there in front of all those teenagers with their attitudes and, well, you know how they are. They are like us a few years ago, but worse."

She manages to make me smile a little.

"Remember Jenna Ford from school?"

I nod. She was an absolute nightmare to the teachers. Always in the remove room. I never went there, of course, but I pictured it as the secondary school equivalent of a padded cell.

"Half the class is like her. And I am a first-year student teacher. You think they listen to me?"

"Even we wouldn't have listened to you." I

manage a smile.

"Exactly. But Vi, this is what I want to do. This is what I have always wanted to do. You know that."

Again, I nod. These are our dreams. This is why we are here.

"So, no matter how many challenging students I meet, I am going to do this. Nothing is going to stop me."

"I'm not you, Zoe. I can't just…"

She cuts me off mid-sentence. "You are not me, but you are Violet Cobham. You are my best friend. You are going to be a midwife. You have worked your ass off to get here. You are not giving up on my best friend's dreams. Not now, not ever."

I snort a big snotty breath and give her a weak, tearful smile.

"You really do overrate me," I say. But every word she says makes me bloom inside. I can feel the warmth of her feelings blossom inside me. So what if Geri thinks I am incapable of succeeding. Zoe, my best friend Zoe, whose opinion matters to me more than anyone else in the world, she thinks I can succeed. No. She knows I can.

"I was going to ask to be given a different placement. Or a different mentor," I say. "But not now. Zoe, I'm going to show her. I am going to show her that I can do it."

"That's it. Put your big girl pants on and show

her."

She reaches over and hugs me, and I try not to wipe my face onto her. When we break free, I dry my eyes again, and face her.

"Is your placement okay then? Will you be alright?" I ask her.

She waves the idea away. "Nothing I can't handle," she says. "Really, it's fine. They are just like us. I mean, a little bit worse, but I remember feeling frustrated and not wanting to be told what to do. It's tough, isn't it?"

"What is?"

"Being a teenager."

I huff a tiny laugh. We are both still eighteen. What we don't know about the world we can make up for through what we know about ourselves, and how much we care about each other.

"It is," I say. "It is."

Chapter Fifteen

The next afternoon, back on my placement, I follow Geri as we check in on the women after handover. I remember how to use the blood pressure machine, and I am sure I do everything she asks exactly as she asks me to do it. Still, her voice is harsh when she talks to me.

The nursing assistant, Ivy, is stripping down a bed in the space next to our final stop of the ward round, and she looks up at me and smiles, giving me a little 'chin up' motion as Geri barks at me.

I want to show my mentor that despite anything she might say to me, I am here to learn, and I am here to succeed. I will do my best until she sees that I am capable and competent. Instead of putting me off, she is driving me to work harder, do better and achieve the very best that I can.

When we have finished the first ward round we go back into the midwives' office. She picks up the heavy steel teapot and pours herself a mug. I am about to sit down next to her when she holds up her hand in a stop sign.

"Go and help Ivy make the beds. You won't know how to fold hospital corners yet, will you?" She doesn't give me a chance to reply. "Now's a good time to learn."

I wouldn't mind a cup of tea too, but instead of

protesting, I say "sure" with a smile on my face and I walk back onto the ward.

In principle, there is nothing wrong with being asked to make beds, and it's true that I need to learn. I still can't help thinking that this is some kind of test or even a punishment. Geri doesn't like me, that much is clear. Whether it's because she doesn't want to be held back by having a student midwife trailing around after her or because I didn't train as a nurse first, I don't know. Either way, it doesn't matter. The fact remains.

There are no other students on the ward. I have no one to share my feelings with. I was looking forward to being here, in the hospital and on the unit, but working with Geri is already feeling emotionally draining.

"Sent you to help, did she?" Ivy asks, as I join her next to the bed.

"We've seen all the ladies," I smile. "Everyone is happy, so I've come to learn how to make a bed."

Ivy hacks out a two-packs a day laugh. "Geri always finds me a helper," she says.

I tilt my head, and wait for her to say more.

"She likes to put her students to work, that's for sure."

It's not just me then, that's almost a relief.

"That's what I'm here for," I say, and as I let the words out, I realise that they are true. What's so wrong with wanting me out here on the ward rather than sitting in the office eating too many biscuits?

Ivy holds out the edge of the clean sheet to me, and I take a corner.

As I make the beds and chat with Ivy, I decide to give my all to this placement. I decide to learn how to work with Geri, and to reflect on what I can gain from working alongside her. If working with Stacey on community taught me the beginnings of the basic skills I need to be a midwife, my placement with Geri can offer me a new depth of understanding. Midwifery is hard work, but being part of a team, learning how to get along with and respect other members of staff is essential.

I've never been afraid of getting my hands dirty, but I will be the first to volunteer when the beds need making, or the bedpans need emptying. I will make the tea at the start of the shift, if no one has beaten me to it, and I will make time to talk to everyone, from consultants to cleaners. Everyone has their role here, and we couldn't work as a whole without each of the unique elements functioning together.

When I return to the midwives' office, there's a mug of tea waiting for me, and Geri hands it over with a smile that I didn't expect.

"Thanks, Violet," she says.

I look at her, accept the tea, and nod.

"It's all part of the learning process." I smile back at her, and I know that everything I do can help me to become a better midwife, even if that might not seem obvious to me at first.

Chapter Sixteen

After six long but rewarding weeks on the postnatal ward, we have a final two-week block in university before Easter break. The excitement of seeing my course mates and catching up on stories from our practice placements is tempered only by the fact that this Friday we will have our first OSCE.

I hope that my scenarios are related to postnatal care. My mind is fresh with the experiences I have had on the Margaret Beresford Unit. If I get a scenario that I have been through in real life, I am sure that I will be fine remembering all the details under examination conditions. If it's something I am less well acquainted with, that will be a different story. The thought of assessors watching my every move, trying to single out anything and everything that I do wrong, is terrifying. Sitting in the first class of the week, I can already feel the first signs of anxiety starting to bite away at me.

"Practice, practice, practice." Rachel Rogers writes the word on the board as she repeats it. "This is your first OSCE. It is the easiest. That's not to say that it is easy, but approaching this test with a positive mindset, after preparing well, will set you in good stead for the remaining OSCEs throughout your course. You can do this. There is nothing in any of the scenarios that you have not been taught about.

There are no trick questions. You should behave exactly as you would do in a real-life situation."

"I'm bricking it," I whisper to Sophie. I hope that she is going to echo my feelings, but instead she gives me a gentle smile.

"You'll be okay, Vi. You know your stuff."

She obviously does, because she doesn't look at all worried. I wish I hadn't said anything. I feel even worse now.

We have gone over the six scenarios exhaustively, and I mean exhaustively, I'm absolutely drained now, and I wish we could get the examination over with. I've got the postnatal placement on my side, half the topics that we have covered are based on postnatal situations. If I get one of those, I will be much more confident.

Behave as you would in a real-life situation. If somehow I can trick my mind into believing that I am on the ward, with an actual pregnant or postpartum patient rather than an actress, maybe I will be able to be the calm, confident student midwife that so far I have managed to be on my placements.

Our exam is on Friday; on Thursday evening I persuade Zoe to stand in as a new mum for me so that I can practice, practice, practice. I've promised her that there's a bottle of gin in it for her afterwards, but tonight we are both keeping a clear head.

I've given Zoe one of the mock scenario sheets that the lecturer posted on the online learning pages, and she is getting into the part with aplomb. She told me to wait outside the bedroom door while she prepared herself, and now it's time for me to enter.

"Hi, Miss Colebrook," I say. It's hard to keep a straight face. Zoe is in the chair next to her desk with one of her pillows stuffed up her t-shirt. It's a very unconvincing fake bump but seeing her like that makes it difficult to control my giggles.

She gives me a stern look.

"You can call me Zoe," she says. She's channelling her inner teacher, and I wonder whether this is what she is like on her placement.

I try my best to straighten up and take this seriously. She is doing me a huge favour, and I need to make the most of this opportunity to practice.

"Thanks, Zoe. So, how are you?"

I ask all the right questions and respond appropriately to her answers. She lies on the bed for me, and even lets me palpate her super-flat tummy. Zoe has always been slim; my chubbiness could pass for a tiny baby belly. It's a good thing she isn't feeling my abdomen. It's difficult to get pregnant when you haven't had sex in…however long it has been.

"Concentrate!" my pretend patient says.

"Sorry, just your tummy is so flat. Hard not to be jealous," I smile.

She bats away the compliment. "So, student midwife Violet, is my imaginary baby growing alright?"

"There's definitely not a baby in there," I say, before snapping back into the role play. "Uh, I mean, yes, Zoe. Everything feels exactly as it should."

She's a great help. I don't know what I would do without her, but even though we spend the rest of the evening practising, there is still that undercurrent of fear that I just can't shake. I know what I am meant to do, I know what I am meant to say, but the thought of performing under exam conditions fills me with dread.

Chapter Seventeen

We have all been given a time slot for our examinations, and unfortunately, I have to wait until afternoon for mine. Zoe is on her placement, but I have come onto campus early anyway. Better to sit in Bradley's and panic than to sit at home and do it; there's better coffee here.

Sophie and Ashley both had their assessments this morning. They were straight onto the group chat, each with their own take on the exam. Ashley thought it was a breeze and took it all in her stride. Sophie forgot her own name when she introduced herself but got into the swing of things once she warmed up. That's almost reassuring.

I can't decide whether it is best to read and reread the notes I have made on the scenarios or whether I should take a break now. Can I try to push too much information into my head? Am I going to get study fatigue? Is that even a thing? I feel like I have learned everything that I am likely to be able to learn now. I still have an hour before the dreaded OSCE. I buy my second latte, then lean back in my chair, stretching my arms and legs, trying to get my blood flowing to them instead of my anxious brain.

All I have done for as long as I can remember is study. My brain is fried. I wasn't planning on sharing that gin with Zoe, but perhaps I will be ready for it after I've finished today. The lecturer told us that learning the scenarios like this is meant to help us to prepare for facing these issues in practice, if we haven't already done so. We will know exactly what to do when we are in real-life situations. I can see where she is coming from, but I wish there were an easier way.

At two fifteen I make my way to the skills lab to wait for my turn. Five minutes early: I figure that's the right balance between not being anxious about getting to the lab late, and not being anxious about having to stand around in the corridor for too long. Either way, by the time I get to the lecture block I can already feel the familiar bubbling of fear in my gut.

When I first started to get anxiety attacks, around seven years ago, my mum took me to the GP. I don't think she knew what to do with me, my mum, that is, not the GP. The GP knew; I suppose they see people like me all the time: panicky, stressed out teenagers who can't keep it together. Of course, I wasn't a teenager then. I was a child, an eleven-year-old child. Instead of putting me straight onto the drugs, I went through counselling and CBT. They didn't help. And then the drugs didn't help either. I didn't feel like myself when I was on them, I felt like I was somewhere else, outside of my body. It was like being a mannequin, just like the ones in the skills lab. I was so tired, but worse than that, I felt empty, dead inside.

And that is why I am standing here now, with sweaty palms and a galloping heartbeat. I choose not to pop the pills that make me feel numb, so I must live with the anxiety that makes me feel petrified.

The door opens and one of the other students walks out. She's smiling, and I take that to be a good sign.

"Good luck," she says, as she passes me.

"Thanks," I just about manage to say. My voice has shrivelled. I need to get back on track before I get into the lab.

"Violet?" Rachel pops her head out of the open door to summon me in.

"Yep." I intend it to sound confident and bold, but it comes out like more of a burp.

"Leave your bag by the door inside and come over to the desk."

She smiles at me; I take a deep breath and walk into the skills lab.

There are a series of cards laid out on the desk, all with their plain sides up. It's a random choice which scenario I will get. Everything is down to me now, which decision I make, and how I handle the scenario that follows. Everything that happens rides on me. I am responsible, I am the only one who can do this, I am going to be sick. I need air. I need to get out of here.

I reach one hand out, meaning to pick up one of the cards, an arbitrary selection, but instead I wobble slightly, and put my hand down on the table instead to stabilise myself.

"Get it together," I say, beneath my breath.

I look around, over my shoulder. Rachel and one of the other lecturers are sitting patiently, waiting for me to make my selection. They say nothing. I turn back to the table. I only have to choose one of these for now. Choose one, play it through, come back for the next. I'll be out of this room in an hour. That's all. I only have to make it through that long.

I can't believe that when I first came into this skills lab, I thought it was just like a hospital room. It has none of the atmosphere, none of the sounds, none of the smells of the ward. There's no undercurrent of chatting, babies crying, phones ringing. There's no baby bath scent, no wet nappy aroma, none of the wafting of hospital meals being delivered to hungry women. Everything feels as false as it actually is. I need to get myself into the right mindset, trick my brain into thinking that this is real.

"Are you ready, Violet? Just choose whichever you like," Rachel calls over.

If I don't get on with it, I'll make the next student late. I would be annoyed if someone had made me wait out there any longer than I had to. I must do this. I have to get on with it now.

I pick up the top left card, and without looking at it, I go over to the lecturers.

Rachel turns it over, and nods. "Lactation and infant feeding," she says. She offers the card back to me, so that I can read the scenario, but the words swim in front of my eyes.

"We will start the examination here, and then move on to the other stations," Rachel says, pointing over to the other side of the skills lab. I can see tables laid out, but my mind can't focus on what they hold.

I stand in front of the woman, smile, and…and nothing. My mind is completely blank. My eyes dart around the room, frantically looking for something, for anything, to prompt me into action, but there is nothing. I am completely frozen.

The woman looks at me with a calm, patient expression as I search for the words that I know I should be saying.

"I…"

Nausea hits me like a punch in the stomach. I'm churning inside. I can't think, I can't think. I can't do anything.

"I'm sorry," I say.

"Take your time, Violet," Rachel says.

Nothing more. No prompts, no hints. I don't need them anyway. I know everything I need to know to pass this examination. I know the basics of infant feeding. I have revised for this scenario, I have seen and heard and advised women on my placements. I know what I should do and what I should say, but when I try to act, I am statue-still. Everything else is spinning. I feel like I am on a merry-go-round, the room swirling around me, the lecturers, this poor woman who has probably never seen anyone react to her like this before, all of it, all of them, everything.

"I…I have to go," I say. "I can't."

"Violet? Are you okay?"

I must look as bad as I feel. I sway a little and put my hands out onto the side of the fake-hospital bed to steady myself.

"I need to go. I'm so sorry."

Rachel is getting to her feet. I wave my hand.

"Really. I'll be okay. It's just…"

I feel so stupid. I don't know what to say. There's nothing I can say to make this any better. All I can do is get out of here.

"Do you want to sit down?"

If I sit, I don't think I will ever get up. I will burst into tears and make even more of an idiot of myself. I shake my head.

"Really, I'm sorry."

I let go of the bed, and without making eye contact with anyone, I walk out of the door.

As soon as I am on the corridor, I break into a run. I don't want my tutor to follow me, to try to make me go back in there. I know that this will mean a big fat fail, but I can't do this. I can't do it. Not now. Maybe not ever.

I can't do it; I can't do it.

I feel deflated, totally drained.

Zoe will still be in her afternoon classes. Part of me wants to message her and ask her to leave her placement and come home with me. I can't do that to her though. It's more than enough that I am messing up my own course, without me ruining her chances of success too.

When I break out of the lecture block into the cold fresh air of the afternoon, I look over to the building that Zoe is usually in. I imagine her sitting at her desk, taking copious amounts of notes, knowing the answers to ever question the lecturer asks. It has always been this way. She has always been the clever one; I've always been the one that messes everything up. Why does she bother hanging around with me? I'll never understand it. I don't deserve her, and I'm sure I don't deserve to be here. There must have been a mistake.

I want to run, to be as far away from here as possible. Being on campus is making my head spin. Why do I have to be so completely useless? When I am on my placements, everything feels so natural. I know what to do. I can talk to women and their families; I can talk to doctors. Working with Geri showed me that I can talk to my superiors, even if they might think that I am only a student, or if they might not appear to value my worth. I felt so good coming out of my postnatal placement, and now, all of that, everything I have learned seems to count for nothing. Now I am back to being the useless, hopeless failure that my dad always told me that I would be.

I thrust my hands deep into my pockets and start to make the walk home, alone. I can feel tears pushing their way into my eyes, but I can't let myself cry here. I'm sure everyone is already staring at me, the sad-faced student moping about on her own. I can't cry. Not here, not now. No matter how much I want to.

Chapter Eighteen

By the time Zoe gets home and runs up to my room, I have had two hours to stew in the thoughts of my failure.

I've changed into leggings and a t-shirt: my lounging-around-feeling-sorry-for-myself outfit. I rarely ever wear anything other than dresses and tights, so as soon as Zoe sees me, she knows that my choice of clothes is not a good sign.

"What happened?" she says. Her eyes are filled with concern. A pang of guilt hits me, like an ice bolt to my heart. I don't want to make her feel bad for me. "You should have texted!"

"I messed up." What else can I say? "I totally bottled it."

"Did you do something wrong, or –"

"I didn't do anything. I stood there and turned to jelly. My brain went to mush, and I couldn't think of a single thing to say."

Zoe frowns and shakes her head. "You were so good in our practice session yesterday. It's not that you can't do it."

"Well, obviously, I can't." The words come out far more bitterly than I mean them to. Zoe ignores my tone though.

"You can. You did everything right last night," Zoe says.

"Last night didn't matter. Today mattered." I practically spit the words. I feel awful about talking to Zoe like this, but I can't seem to stop myself. She is doing her best, I know she is.

She looks down at her feet. I suppose she is trying to think of something reassuring to say to me. There's nothing that can make me feel better.

"Look, I'm going to run a bath and stew for a while, okay? I appreciate you're trying to help, but I think I need some time alone to get my head around things."

She nods and doesn't speak.

"I'm sorry for being an idiot," I say.

"You're really not, but okay," she says. "See you downstairs later?"

"Yeah."

I don't know whether I will feel like company, but it's always reassuring to know she is there for me. It's not often that I want to be alone. I don't like big crowds, or having a lot of people around me, but it's rare that I don't want to be with Zoe. It's not her personally that I don't want to be with; I need to be alone right now. I've messed up something that is incredibly important, and I only have myself to blame.

Before she turns to leave, she says, "Don't beat yourself up about this. It's going to be okay."

I don't know what else to say, but she hovers in

the doorway until I give her a tight-lipped, obviously fake smile. I hate feeling like this. I hate being like this.

Hiding in the bathroom was one of my coping strategies when my mum and dad used to argue. Even if I were in my bedroom, their fights would always escalate to the point where I would be dragged in, like some kind of referee, or someone to cast the deciding vote.

"What do you think, Violet? Is your mother lazy?"

"Do you think she does enough around the house?"

"Are your friends' mothers like this?"

And, of course, that all time classic:

"Would you rather be with your mum or me?"

My dad. It was always my dad saying those things. Mum would stand looking embarrassed; I suppose she always knew that it was wrong to involve me in their fights. She wasn't strong enough to get out and get away from them though. Not then, at least.

If I ran a bath, locked the door, and lay in the tub, I would be left alone. They never disturbed me there. It was like a sacred place. I always felt safe in the bathroom, I suppose it still is my safe place. It's where I go to be alone, to relax and unwind.

I know that I have my own bedroom here, and I

can shut my door and ask for some time or space or whatever, and Zoe will respect that, but I feel awful turning her away, or shutting her out. If I am in the bath, she knows not to disturb me; it's an unwritten rule of our friendship. I come in here and lock the door, but I am locking myself in rather than locking her out.

Slipping beneath the warm water, my mind begins to clear. I have to find a way to deal with my anxiety. If it is going to affect my course like this, I have to start to consider my options. Should I go back to the GP? I don't think I could handle medications again; all they did was make me feel a different kind of bad. There are probably different therapies that I could try, but last time was awful. The thought of it turns my stomach. I can't do that again. I was practically a zombie; I certainly wasn't myself.

Counselling then? Cognitive behaviour therapy? Self-help? Isn't that what I have been doing? Getting through by helping myself? By having Zoe help me? Perhaps it's time to see a professional, or at least talk to my tutor, the support services or someone. All of those options though, they make me feel like a failure, like I am not strong enough to deal with my life on my own. They make me feel like a failure. I don't think I am ready to label myself. Can I get through this on my own?

When I finally make it downstairs, I run through my thoughts with Zoe.

"You're not on your own," she says.

It's only eight o'clock, but I'm in my pyjamas, in the living room. Zoe and Luke are both on the sofa. I wasn't sure whether I should discuss my anxiety in front of him, but I guess he is my friend now, he may as well know the real me.

"I know," I say. "I mean without professional help. Or drugs. That kind of alone."

"They were pretty crappy when you took them before." She shudders as she speaks.

I'm sure Zoe remembers as clearly as I do what happened the last time I took the meds. Perhaps she remembers even more clearly, having been on the outside looking in.

"What happens now? About your exam?" Ever practical, Luke brings us back to the fundamentals.

"I got a message from Rachel, the module leader. I have to go and see her on Monday morning." It's my turn to shudder now. I have no idea how I am going to make myself go to her office.

"You have two full days to think through your options," he says. "Try to be logical and pragmatic."

"Us girls are emotional and unpredictable, Luke. Being logical and pragmatic is too difficult for us." I tilt my head as I deal out my snarky response.

He doesn't bite at the bait. "It's a good thing that

you have another viewpoint here then. If you keep thinking about how you messed up, or how bad you think you are - and Violet, you really are not - you're going to drive yourself nuts over the weekend. Make a plan. Decide what you are going to do. You can't change what happened today, but you can change what you do in future."

"You think I should get help then?" I say, still on the defensive.

"I'm not saying that you should do that, no. I'm saying that you should decide what you want to do. Think about the pros and cons."

Zoe looks at me and shrugs. "That seems like a sensible suggestion."

I ease back into the armchair, starting to feel more relaxed. Having control of my future and starting to get control of my anxiety would be a step in the right direction, that's for sure. Maybe Luke is right.

Chapter Nineteen

On Monday morning, the last week of term, I am standing outside Rachel's room. My mind is racing, trying to work out what I should say to her. Is there any way I can mitigate the way I acted in the examination? I cannot think of anything I can tell her that will make this any better.

She calls me in and gets straight to the point.

"You need to pass the resit to get through to the second year. There is no way around it. There's no way to substitute grades from another module or take an average mark forward." She looks at my file and nods her head. "You have achieved excellent grades so far. Your assignment results in the first term were all above sixty percent. That tells me that you are capable. What happened?"

"I clammed up. I had a massive anxiety attack and…" I throw my hands in the air. There's no way of explaining how I felt that she will understand.

"Do you have any medication, or have you received any support for this?"

"No. When I first started getting the attacks my mum took me to see someone, I mean my doctor. They gave me some tablets, but they didn't help. I stopped taking them. Why take something if it doesn't make you feel any better?" I'm bored of going over this now. I don't particularly want to talk about it again, but I understand why she needs to know.

"That makes sense," Rachel says. "But this is your future on the line. I want to make sure that you are as prepared as possible for your resit. It might be worth you contacting the Learning Support Service, and maybe you should ask your GP for some advice?"

I gulp, but the lump I feel in my throat remains firmly in place.

"Okay." I say the word quietly. I really don't want to take drugs again. I am not sure that it will help. I have to pass this module though. Without getting through the resit, I can't continue.

"If you don't mind sharing your details, there is another student in the group that needs to resit, and it might be worth the two of you running through some scenarios together to practice."

That sounds like a solution that I can get behind. My voice is firmer when I say "okay" this time.

"Chin up, Violet. You are not the first student to fail the OSCE and you will most certainly not be the last. See it as an additional opportunity to review your skills and knowledge."

An opportunity. It didn't feel like that at the time. Can I really put myself through that again? The bottom line is that I must if I want to continue.

I want to continue.

I have to do this.

I did think things through, over the weekend. I went over and over it in my head. I know that everyone only wants what is best for me, and that Zoe, Luke, and Rachel, all my mentors, everyone, they all want me to succeed. I have never had so much support before. I don't deserve all these lovely people backing me. What I do know is that having their support makes me want to succeed. I want to beat anxiety and although it might be a ridiculous thing to think – I want to do it on my own. I don't want the drugs that deaden me; I don't want therapy. I want the satisfaction of beating this.

"Make a plan," Luke said.

That's what I have done. I have thought it through all weekend, and my plan is to kick anxiety's butt. I can do it. I have to. I don't get those feelings when I am on placement; when I have my uniform on and I'm in the heat of the action I know what to do and when to do it. That must mean that I am capable, I am able to beat this. I'm going to give it my best shot.

Chapter Twenty

Returning to uni after Easter break is bittersweet. On one hand I am finally about to start my first delivery suite placement. On the other hand, the prospect of resitting my OSCE is looming over me like a dark cloud. I'm trying to be positive, but If I don't pass, this is the end for me. No third chances, I will be out. I can't let that happen.

It's mid-April, my resit isn't until the second week of June. I wish I could do it straight away, get it over with. I wish I hadn't failed in the first place.

I have all this term's work to do in addition to my resit. I need to focus. Everything I have dreamed of rides on passing my OSCE. Nothing else matters. It's the final term of the first year. If I want to make it through to the second, I must pass.

Sunday evening, the day before start of term, the mood in the house is ice-cold. Zoe and I arrived back this afternoon, and, just like after the Christmas break, there's been no sign of Luke.

"Must be with that girl again," Zoe says.

"Hmm. Yeah." I should be more supportive, I know, but my thoughts are elsewhere.

"Should have expected it, I suppose." She's curled up on the sofa, I'm in my usual armchair. We have so far managed to eat dinner and binge watch half of a new series that's based on a book we both read last year. Neither of us is motivated to do much else, it seems.

"Yeah," I say again. I can't remember anything I just watched on the television. Snap out of it. Come on. I look at Zoe. "I'm sorry," I say. "I know you really like him. I don't know what –"

Before I can carry on with the sentence, I hear the footfall on the stairs that can only mean one thing. If Andrew hasn't turned up, Luke must be home. He's been here all along, and neither of us realised.

Zoe and I pass a shared look of surprised confusion. I click pause on the remote, and we listen, waiting for him to come in and join us. There's a thud of footsteps heading into the kitchen, the clunk of the fridge opening, and another as it closes, and then the steps head back, through the hall and up the stairs.

He must know that we are in here; neither of us has been particularly quiet. The television has been on, and we weren't exactly listening quietly.

"Maybe she is with him?" Zoe says in a loud whisper. Her face is stricken; she sits up.

"Do you think so? I guess that would explain him not coming down."

"Oh no, oh no. I don't want to…" she trails off. "Vi, I couldn't."

All thoughts I had of the forthcoming stressful term fade away as I turn my focus to my best friend.

I can't bear seeing her like this.

"Zo, I'm so sorry that things haven't worked out the way you wanted them to," I say.

"I should have said something before Christmas. I shouldn't have waited. I'm such an idiot."

"You thought you had time," I say. "Everything was going so well between you. Taking it slowly is the best way, right?"

I don't know if that's true or not. I know so little about relationships that it is impossible for me to give Zoe any real, practical advice. My last relationship was six months ago, and it only existed for two months. What do I know?

Jared Clarke. Tall, dark, and useless, as it turned out. Before that there was Charlie Nunn, my first, and only, love. I don't still love him, he's not my only love in the one-true-love of my life sense. He's my only love because he is the only man, boy, that I have ever loved. Yet. Eighteen months on, I know that I will find someone else. One day. When I am ready. Right now? I couldn't care less. My world is uni, and Zoe. I don't need anything else.

"I thought that if we kept getting to know each other then things might naturally progress." She runs her fingers through her long red hair and lets it fall over her face like a veil. "I'm so stupid."

"He's stupid not to have snapped you up," I say. I don't know what else I can do to make her feel better.

"What if he brings her down to introduce her to us? What then? I think I'll probably flip out." She tosses her head in a melodramatic flounce.

"You will do what you always do. You'll be cool and calm. You'll politely say hello and you will probably end up making friends with her, because that's the kind of person you are. You can't dislike anyone. Not really. You're too nice, Zo."

She smiles at this and gestures at me to restart the television programme.

"Let's not think about bad things," she says. "Let's watch the end of this and then break out the gin."

"A sound idea, Miss Colebrook." I smile.

"That's what the kids call me." She laughs, and we both settle to watch Netflix and try to not think about bad things.

When we don't see Luke at breakfast, we agree that our assumption was most probably right. I give Zoe a hug before we part company for our separate lectures, but I still carry with me the sadness that she is feeling.

Ashley has been to a midwifery conference over the Easter break and she enthuses about it from the moment I sit next to her to when our lecturer arrives to start the session. I try to concentrate, but my thoughts keep turning back to my friend, and what I can possibly do to help her.

I decide to make Zoe's favourite dinner to cheer her up. By six o'clock, two bowls of steaming pasta with a hashed-up tomato type sauce sit on the table. A glass of wine each. A loaf of piping hot garlic bread. I cooked, and Zoe opened the wine. It seems like a fair deal. We are just about to get stuck in when the door opens, and Luke comes in.

"Smells great," he says. Just that. No hello, no explanation of where he has been or what happened yesterday. Certainly no sign of a girl. His voice isn't quite its usual chirpy tone though; something seems a little out of sync.

"There's more in the pan, if you want some." Zoe nods her head in the direction of the hob. There's no trace of emotion in her voice. I'm impressed with her control.

"Thanks." Luke's voice is dull and flat, like cardboard that has been left out in the garden.

"You okay?" I ask. I think about leaving it there, but I bite the bullet and continue anyway. "We didn't want to disturb you last night."

He raises his head in a little jerk. "Yeah." He walks over to get himself some of the pasta, giving Zoe and I the chance to look at each other, sharing a bewildered exchange of glances. Something is going on, that's the only thing of which I am certain.

I lift my fork and start to eat, but it tastes bland now.

Luke hovers by the table and I think for a moment that he is going to take his food and go upstairs. I kick his chair back slightly, hoping it will encourage him to sit.

Throughout, Zoe is silent. She has taken a large swig of her wine though.

Luke puts his bowl onto the table and stirs the pasta and sauce together. Without looking at either of us, he scoops some into his mouth, swallows, and repeats.

"Lovely dinner Vi," Zoe says. I nod; I'm forcing myself to keep eating. "Thanks for this."

The atmosphere hangs thick like fog, and I almost wish that Luke hadn't joined us. The three of us eat on in silence as the ambience freezes.

I leave it until I have almost finished my food, but I can't take it anymore.

"Do you want to talk about it?" I say. I put down my cutlery and look at Luke. "I'm not sure I can bear this silence. What's happened?"

Zoe coughs and almost chokes on the piece of garlic bread that she is chewing. I hand her wine to her, and nod at her to drink.

Luke looks from me to her and then back down into his bowl.

"I don't want to talk about it. No." He drops his fork, pushes himself back from the table and walks out, up the stairs, to his room.

Zoe raises her eyebrows. "Well done, Violet."

"Oh, what was I supposed to do? That was painful. You didn't want to ask because…" I stop myself. I don't want to get into an argument with Zoe, but we both know the reason that she didn't want to ask Luke what was wrong. "Forget it," I say. "I probably had too much wine." The truth is, I haven't touched a drop yet.

Chapter Twenty-One

Community, postnatal and antenatal are all as much a part of maternity care as intrapartum, but there's something special about delivery suite. When I first started to dream of being a midwife it was being present with women during childbirth that drew me in. I wanted to be a part of something emotional, intimate, and intense. I wanted to support women to have the best experiences of that time that they possibly could. That was my starting point. As I became more aware, read more about midwifery and found out as much as I could about the career, I realised that what midwives do during the antenatal and postnatal periods can have a massive effect upon women's emotional and physical wellbeing too. Every action matters. Every interaction matters. Even today, coming to the end of only my first year of training, I know that.

Still, today is my first day on delivery suite, and if I told you that this is just the same as any other placement, I would be lying. I desperately want to see a baby being born. It's hard to explain what an amazing experience that will be. I have sat in class with Ashley, Simon, and Sophie, and heard stories from their placements. Simon was present at a birth in the first term; he got lucky when his community placement mentor was called into delivery suite.

Ashley had her delivery suite allocation last term, so she has already seen five births, and helped with two deliveries. I feel like I am lagging already.

Instead of anxiety, my chest flutters with excitement as I push open the double doors of the delivery suite. The long corridor stretches past closed doors to the midwives' station, and behind it the staff room. Am I meant to leave my bag somewhere? Are there lockers for my coat? Where do I find my mentor?

The last question is the first to be answered. "Violet?"

I nod. I must stand out as the newbie, turning up in my grey and navy, fresh and eager to be here.

"Hi," I say.

"I'm Jade." She holds out her hand, formally. "I'm your mentor."

"Hi," I say again. I realise that I am repeating myself and superfluously add "Hello". I must be bright red; I can feel it in my cheeks.

"Let me take you to the locker room quickly, then we'll get into handover. We have a few minutes. I'll show you around once the night shift have left, okay?"

I try to speak, and my voice comes out like a mouse squeak. Jade leads me along the corridor, past a further line of closed doors, and around a corner into a locked changing room.

"You can wear theatre blues on the ward if you want to. It can get a little messy at times." She waves to a set of shelves stacked with neat piles of azure blue tops and pants in various, labelled, sizes.

"Okay," I say. "Thanks." I'll stay in my uniform today though. I want everyone to know that I am a new student and I have no idea what I am doing. If I wear my uniform, I hope I won't be asked to do anything or fetch anything that I haven't a clue about. I don't want people to rely on me just yet, not while I am floundering around like a fish out of water.

There is a line of lockers, and Jade pulls one open for me so I can put my bag inside.

"Leave your coat on any of the hooks. It will be fine here. No mobile phones on the ward. Make sure it's turned off and placed in your locker."

I reach back into my bag and slide my phone off. It will be weird not having it by my side, but perhaps the break will do me good. I can live without social media for a few hours, and Zoe will just have to wait to hear about how exciting or how terrible my day is. I hope that it will turn out to be the former.

We go back up to the staff room in time for handover. On the wall is a large dry-wipe board, with nine rows outlined in what appears to be black tape. Down the side of the board is a column listing the initials of the doctors on call, the obstetricians, the paediatricians, and the anaesthetic team. I recognise some of the names from my spell on postnatal. It's reassuring to have at least something recognisable, because everything else flashes around me in a blur of new and unfamiliar.

There are three women's names listed in the rows, and beside each name are a string of numbers and letters. I don't need to try to decipher them, because the midwife in charge starts handover, and everything quickly becomes apparent.

"Angela Flint, thirty-two years old primigravida. Thirty-eight weeks. Induction of labour for pre-eclampsia." She reels off Ms Flint's vital signs, the medication she has had so far, and the general plan of care.

The other two women are Naomi Whyte, who has come in for a check in 'query early labour' and Michelle Staples who thinks her waters might have broken. Neither of them is in established labour yet, and the midwife in charge seems to think they will be discharged home soon.

"There's another induction on antenatal ward, nothing happening yet, and we sent a multip home a couple of hours ago. She came in with irregular contractions, didn't phone first." There's a collective sigh. "Not in labour, but who knows? She knows to phone and come in when she needs to. Okay, nothing else to report."

The midwife taking charge of the afternoon shift writes on the board and then looks around the room at the staff who will be joining her. She directs her attention to me.

"So, it's your first shift?" she asks, and I nod. "Okay, well Jade, you and Violet take room three."

The induction. I can't hold back my smile. I don't focus on the rest of the allocations; my mind is already on the possibility that I might see a birth on my very first shift on delivery.

After the midwife in charge finishes speaking, a brown-haired midwife with cute glasses comes over to talk to us.

"Hi Violet. Welcome to delivery suite. I'm Emma. I was looking after Angela this morning."

"Hi Emma," I say. My voice seems to be getting back to normal now that it has had time to settle, or now I am getting my excitement under control.

Emma directs most of what she is saying to Jade, but occasionally glances at me to keep me included. I like her already. "Her blood pressure has been fairly stable." She opens the notes to show the chart that tracks all the vital signs during labour. Midwives call this the partogram. I like the name. I like the not-so-secret language that we share, the language of childbirth. We have words and phrases that we would not usually use outside of the maternity world. Primigravida, a first-time mother, also known as a primip (short for primipara). Multip, or multigravida, someone who has been pregnant or given birth before. Pre-eclampsia, well I wish we didn't have to know that one. It's a pregnancy disorder that is characterised mainly by high blood pressure and protein in the urine. If left uncontrolled or untreated it can lead to eclampsia, hence the name. Eclampsia can be lethal for mother and baby, so the trick is to spot it and treat it before it escalates.

"She's having a few contractions, but nothing regular yet. CTG has been fine."

CTG, there's another midwifery term. The cardiotocograph – a recording of the baby's heartbeat and activity of the mother's uterus. I haven't used one of those yet. In clinic we listened to babies' heartbeats through a handheld electronic machine called a Doppler, or the old school way, using a wooden cone called a Pinard. It's amazing how many tools of the trade there are for something as natural as childbirth. Once you start to introduce drugs to start contractions in an induction and add continuous monitoring with a CTG machine, things really aren't all that natural at all anymore. I wonder how many births I will attend that are 'natural' in the way that I think of it.

Emma leads the way into room three, and Jade

and I follow behind.

Mum-to-be Angela is sitting up on the bed, dressed in an oversized nightshirt and covered from the waist down with a thin white sheet. Her brown hair is pulled up into a messy topknot.

There's an IV line connected to a cannula in her left hand, and two wires pop above the sheet and connect to the cardiotocograph monitor by the side of her bed that is providing a trace of the baby's heart rate.

"Hi Angela, this is Jade, and Violet, a student midwife, who will be looking after you this afternoon." Emma smiles, and I say hello.

As she finishes speaking, Angela's expression starts to change. Her face tightens, and she reaches down to grab the bar on the side of the bed.

"Contraction?" Emma asks.

Angela nods rapidly. Jade walks over to the side of the bed, but before she gets there the contraction has ended.

"They aren't lasting long," Angela says. "It's fine."

"Is your husband with you?" Jade asks.

"He's at work," Angela shrugs. "I'm okay. He's not far away, he can come at short notice."

"I'm going to leave you with Jade and Violet now," says Emma. "I hope you get going soon and have an easy labour.

"Thanks for this morning," Angela says. "Come and see us when we make it upstairs"

"I will," Emma smiles and leaves the three of us.

I don't know what to do or say, so I stand, trying to look friendly, calm, and approachable.

Jade seems completely at ease. She runs through a series of checks.

"We need to have a baseline at the beginning of the shift," she says, showing me everything that she is doing and chatting to Angela at the same time.

It seems almost automatic to her, yet there is nothing conveyer belt like about her approach. There's such a lot to take in. I wonder if I will ever be able to appear this comfortable and confident. All I can do today is whatever I can to make Angela's birth day as positive as possible.

Chapter Twenty-Two

By the end of my first shift on delivery suite I haven't seen a birth. Jade and I supported Angela throughout the day, but by the time our shift finished at half past nine Angela was five centimetres dilated. Her contractions were strong and regular, and she was in established labour, but delivery was unlikely to happen until well into the nightshift.

I spent most of the shift chatting to Angela, not as a patient, not discussing only baby names and birth plans, but talking about life the universe and everything. I felt like I had a purpose, above being a student midwife, there to watch; I felt like I was learning more than how to listen to the baby's heartrate and monitor contractions. Still, a part of me is disappointed that I didn't get to see Angela's baby come into the world.

Tuesday's shift comes and goes with no sign of a delivery; I'm trying to be patient; I know that midwifery is about more than catching babies – even on delivery suite. I'm on a late shift on Wednesday. Zoe is out on her placement, so I have the morning to kill at Tangiers Court without her.

I'm so used to getting up early now that I don't even bother to plan a lie in. My schedule involves breakfast, a long, hot bath and then a little bit of reading before I get ready to go to my placement. As with all the best laid plans though, things are not turning out as I had expected.

I'm waiting for the kettle to boil for my first coffee of the day when Luke stumbles into the kitchen.

"No lectures today?" he asks.

"Placements," I say. "First week on delivery suite."

"Nice. Have you delivered any babies yet?" He walks over and pulls a mug out of the cupboard and puts it down next to mine.

"Not yet. It's my third shift today. They don't let us get stuck in straight away."

"See one do one?" he smiles.

I put a spoonful of coffee granules into his mug. "See five, do one, but you weren't far off."

"How hard can it be?" he says. "People in Africa give birth in the bushes, don't they?"

I've heard this before, unsurprisingly. "Well, yes. And a lot of them have some serious problems."

This gets his interest, but I'm not really in much of a mood to start a discussion about potential pregnancy and birth complications right now. He looks at me expectantly.

"You'll have to switch to my course if you want to find out more," I say.

"I don't think that they allow a straight swap from

accountancy to midwifery, but I could ask."

I tilt my head and smile. "Sure," I say.

"Men don't study midwifery, anyway, do they?" he asks.

"Not as many men as women, sure. We have a future male midwife on the course though."

A look of surprise crosses his face. "Not sure why a man would want to be a midwife."

"I'm not sure why a man would want to be an accountant, but there you go." I like teasing him; he's a fun target.

He picks up the spoon and bops me gently on the forehead with it. "Round one to the scientist."

The kettle clicks and I make the coffee. Luke passes me the milk from the fridge and puts it away again after I have added a splash to each of our cups.

"Teamwork," he says.

Luke appears to be in a much better mood than he has been since he came back from Leeds. I take a sip of my coffee. The text on the mug says, 'I'd agree with you but then we'd both be wrong'. The drink's too hot, and I withdraw sharply.

"Careful there. What are your plans? Want to watch TV or something?"

"We could just chat if you like?" I gesture towards the chairs at the little round table.

He pauses, considering the idea carefully. It is as though I opened a window; a cold chill passes between us.

"Okay," he says, simply. He takes a seat, and I sit beside him.

Looking at my mug, reading the humorous slogan over and over, it seems like forever before he speaks.

"We're friends, aren't we, Violet?" he says.

It's not what I expected, and I start a little in surprise.

"Uh, of course, yes. Why?"

"Well, this isn't the sort of thing I talk about. I mean, I know men aren't known for discussing their emotions and all that, but I don't have any friends that I could talk about them with if I wanted to. I have friends, of course I do, but apart from you and Zoe they are all guys. And we really don't talk about feelings."

There's a heavy lump in my throat. Countless thoughts flash through my mind as I try to imagine what he is about to tell me. Feelings? What kind of feelings? About whom? Why would he talk to me about feelings?

"I'm a good listener." I smile and carefully take a small sip of my coffee. It's started to cool. "You have to be in my line of work, right?"

He nods but doesn't return the smile.

"Okay," he says. "I'm not sure that I am a good talker, but I'll try."

I shuffle around in my seat to get comfortable and

give him my full attention, and then I am silent as I let him speak.

"The girl I was seeing, back home. It's all turned out to be a bit of a disaster."

I take another sip and say nothing.

"I didn't really want to go into it all with you two. You don't need to hear about my, er, issues." He runs his hand through his dark, unruly hair and continues. "I used to date her back in college. Over the summer, we agreed that a long-distance thing wasn't going to work. I mean she decided, and I couldn't persuade her otherwise, so I had to agree really. It wasn't what I wanted."

"First love?" I ask, trying to make my interest sound like nonchalance.

"Kind of. I'm not sure I know what 'love' is yet, really. I liked her a lot though. I thought we had a future. We were together for eight months. December to August, okay, nine months. Then one day she says that we need to talk, and I know what's coming. I'm going to Wessex University, she's going to Aberdeen, and it's a long way between the two." He pauses again. "I told her I could get a plane up or something. We could have made it work." He looks genuinely crestfallen.

"So, you split up, and came here."

"Yeah. I tried to put her behind me. I got on with my studying and thought about her as little as possible."

"Then you saw her at Christmas?"

"Then…yeah. I was out with my mates, and she showed up. More beautiful than I even remembered her. She really is a stunner, you know. All curves and curls and…I don't want to think about that." He shakes his head, as if trying to shake the image out of his mind. "We had a few drinks and she asked me to go back to hers." He looks at me, with a sheepish expression. "What was I meant to do?"

I raise my hands in a tiny shrug gesture.

"Well, I said no, actually." He smiles at me, as if he has tricked me into thinking badly of him. "I told her that I couldn't do it. I wasn't prepared to get hurt again. I sound stupid, don't I?"

"Not at all. It sounds far from stupid." I say.

"We met up the next day and talked everything through. She told me how much she missed me, and it seemed too good to be true. She'd made a mistake letting me go, she said. Couldn't go on without me, all that stuff."

"So, you got back together."

"So, we got back together. Only after she promised that this was it, that she was committing to make it work and she wouldn't bail on me again. I told her that I couldn't go through that, Violet."

I never imagined that Luke could be so sensitive and vulnerable. I haven't seen this side of him before. Six months we have lived in this house together, and I know so little about him.

"I understand," I say.

"I couldn't wait to get home for Easter. All I could think about was seeing her again."

I frown. "What happened?"

"I hadn't been home more than an hour; I hadn't even had chance to go round to see her. Her sister turns up on my doorstep."

I must look very confused at this point.

"I know her from visiting Kelly, of course. That's her name. Kelly. I know her sister, sure. And when I saw her standing there, I got a sick feeling in my gut. I knew it wasn't going to be anything good."

"Kelly. Is she okay? Is…"

He stops me talking with a dark laugh.

"She is absolutely fine. Her sister wanted to let me in on a few home truths before I made a complete fool of myself. 'Kelly has been carrying on with someone up in Aberdeen,' she told me. No wonder Kell didn't want me to go up there to visit her. She texted me, we did all the naughty phone stuff, but as soon as I mentioned going up to see her, she told me to wait until Easter, wait until we could be together again. All that time, she was with some other guy." His expression is a mix of anger and pain. I put my hand onto his wrist.

"That's awful, I'm sorry, Luke."

"I wanted to be home so much. I wanted to see her, be with her, but after that, all I wanted was to be back here, as far away from her as possible."

"Did she try to, I don't know, lie about it? Cover it up?"

"Not once her sister told me, no. At least she was honest after she got found out. I don't think she's thanking her sister for telling me though."

"No," I say. "Her sister did the right thing though, for whatever reason."

He laughs. "She said that she wanted Kelly to do the right thing too. Is that what it was? It didn't feel right. Nothing about it did."

"It's really rubbish. Sorry, Luke."

We look at our mugs, not speaking.

"It feels good to get it out though," he says eventually. "Thanks."

I nod. "Sure. Sorry I can't say much helpful."

"There's nothing that can help. I learned a lesson. Never trust anyone."

"I'm not sure that is your take home message from this." I frantically think of something to say to change his mind. Things might not have worked out with Kelly, but now there is a chance for Zoe. If there's anything I can do to keep his faith in womankind alive, I have to do it.

"She's not every woman, she is one woman. Just because she did this to you doesn't mean that every woman will."

"Well, I don't believe in second chances. I won't be seeing Kelly again. I don't think I want to see anyone. Not for a while."

"Hmm." I can't stop myself from nodding. "I know that feeling."

"Something similar happen to you?" he asks.

I think for a few moments. "Not similar, no. Someone broke up with me, and then wanted me to take him back when he felt like it. I said no." I shrug and drain the rest of my coffee. "I thought that being alone was better than being unhappy with someone."

"Tangiers Court. Home of the Singles Club." He manages a smile as he says it.

"Andrew is probably off in a harem somewhere, living the life for all of us."

"Ah. Let him have it. We have books, coffee and…actually, yeah. Pretty sad, aren't we?"

I start to laugh along with him. It's kind of funny, but somewhere inside, I do feel that there might just be some truth in what he has said.

Chapter Twenty-Three

As I take the bus to the hospital for my afternoon shift, I send Zoe a text message.

Had a chat with Luke. Lots to tell you xx

I expect a rapid reply, but then I check the time and realise that she is likely to be in class, and away from her phone. On one hand, Luke is single and available now, on the other, he seems to be resolutely done with relationships for the time being. I don't know that this is going to feel like good news to Zoe. Still, at least she has a chance now.

I have to put my belongings in the locker again when I get to the ward, so there's no possibility of continuing our conversation until break time. When I am working my mind never has the opportunity to miss social contact. I focus on the women I am caring for or the tasks that I need to carry out. Still, today I wish I could talk to Zoe.

On my lunch break I pop back into the locker room. I sit on the wooden bench, between the hanging jackets, and turn my phone on. It takes a few seconds to glow back into life after its morning of sleep. When the data signal kicks in there are three messages from Zoe. It's half past twelve now, she should be on her lunch break too. I click on the notifications and read her messages.

Can't leave you alone, can I? :) Tell me everything xx

Ten minutes later

You're on the ward, aren't you? This is agonising! Message me as soon as you read this! xx

Immediately followed by

Unless it is bad news. I don't want bad news. Tell me something good! xx

I have to put her out of her misery. I try to think of the best way to phrase things in a quick text message.

He's split up with the girl. She was no good. Will explain all later. Could be your chance! xx

I re-read the message and click SEND. It will do for now. There's only so much you can say in a message. Much as I love texting, sometimes it feels so limited.

I sit a little longer, the overhead strip light buzzes softly to itself, and being here in the locker rooms feels like I am in a cocoon. It's a pod of calm in an otherwise hectic and noisy ward. I make a mental note to come and sit here again in future when I need some space. I've settled into the peacefulness when my phone buzzes in my hand. I almost let it slip through my fingers, but I grasp it just in time.

WHAT? TELL ME EVERYTHING! XXX

All capitals. Extra kiss. Yep, she is definitely

excited.

Be home before you. Coffee shop when you finish? xx

It's not a conversation I want Luke to walk in on. There's a cute indie coffee shop on the high street that we have never quite managed to stop by, and I feel like today is the day.

By five o'clock we've got home, changed, and excitedly bustled our way into Blackheath's café. It's a super-cute boutique coffee shop with mismatched chairs and heavy old wooden tables, a far cry from the franchised chains that seem to have invaded the town centre. Latte for me and a mocha, extra shot, extra hot for Zoe. We find seats in the corner and I can finally start to tell her about my conversation with Luke.

I spill everything that he told me, and watch her expression turn from curiosity to compassion to confusion.

"Where does that leave me?" she says.

"I really don't know." It's the truth. I hope that the two of them will somehow get it together now, but if he is intent on staying single, should she try to persuade him otherwise? Should I even encourage her? She's Zoe. She's my best friend. Whatever she wants, I will always support her.

"I was kicking myself after Christmas for waiting

too long and letting someone else snap him up," she says. "I don't know if I can be patient and let that happen again."

"Snap him up," I laugh. "Like he's a bargain in the January sales."

She smiles and nudges me. "You know what I mean."

I do, of course.

"As you know very well, I am far from an expert on these things," I say. "Asking me about love is like asking an atheist about religion. I have no idea. I don't know anything about how men's brains work."

"I have trouble understanding how my own brain works some days," she says. She holds onto her coffee cup, staring into it as if the answers to all her questions are somewhere in the milky drink.

"You can either tell him how you feel or wait and see what happens. If it's meant to be, it will be, right? I mean, you both get on so well, and…"

"You and he get on well too. We are all friends, aren't we? That's the thing. Maybe he is just a nice person who gets on with everyone, and I am wasting my time dreaming about being with him."

"Newsflash, Zo. You are a really nice person who gets on well with everyone too."

"You have to say that; you're my best friend."

"Well, yes, you've got me there." I give her a wink.

It's all true though. Zoe isn't simply my best friend, and my favourite human that I have ever met, she is genuinely a great person that everyone likes. Everyone. When we were in school together, everyone talked to her, from the cliques to the geeks. There's something about her that people seem to be attracted to. I just float along by her side being my wobbly, anxious, imperfect self.

"Well, if he's plumping for the bachelor life for a while, I probably don't have to rush anything." She lets out a light sigh. "You must have had enough of me going on about him."

"It's fine, really. Not like I have anyone to go on about, is it?"

"If you wanted to meet someone, I know that you would. You've never had a problem finding gorgeous guys to fall at your feet."

"Hmm." I put my mug down and stare at it. "Gorgeous but brainless."

"We are at university. If you want brains, you came to the right place."

I shudder slightly. "Yeah. No. I mean, not yet. It'll happen when it happens."

Meeting someone is still very close to the bottom of my to-do list. At the top is getting through the year, passing my resit, and seeing Zoe happy. If those things happen, life will be perfect.

Chapter Twenty-Four

I'm not having much luck on delivery suite. I know that I am not here to simply witness births, and eventually start delivering babies, but two weeks into my placement I have yet to see a baby being born. Either the women that I care for don't get anywhere near to delivery during my shifts, or there aren't any labouring women on the unit when I am here. The excited buzz that I felt when I started this placement has settled to a flat feeling, like the bubbles have been let out of my bottle.

I'm trying to focus on the positives. I have had some experience of being with women and their partners during labour. It's something that I hadn't anticipated being quite as emotional as I have found it. Seeing couples together like that, men supporting their partners, there's something about it. It's hard to explain if you haven't experienced it. Of course, there are women who don't come in with a man, but so far, I have only met couples, and male-female couples at that. My experiences have been extremely limited, but even without having seen a birth, I am still enjoying every day here.

The postnatal ward was busy every day. There was always something to do, especially seeing as Geri loved to keep me on my toes. Here on delivery, there are long lulls where no women's names are written on the board. Today is my tenth shift, I have a very small sample size to work with. I've spent the first hour and a half today going through my PAD with Jade.

I'm walking up the ward, carrying a tray of empty mugs and a huge metal teapot when I hear the phone ringing. Chloe, the midwife in charge of today's shift is at the desk, chatting to one of the junior doctors. She scoops the handset up and answers.

"Delivery suite, Sister Brookes, can I help you?"

I set the tray down in the staff room and keep an ear on the phone conversation. Incoming calls can lead to incoming patients, and I hope that, eventually, incoming patients will give birth. I flick my eyes up to the clock. I have another six hours on the ward today. That's plenty of time. I can hear Chloe talking.

"Can I speak to your wife? I know, but if she can talk to me, yes, that's great thanks. Elizabeth? Hello. So, what has been happening? Okay. And how often are these pains coming now? Right," I can hear the scratch of her pen against the paper in the call log. We write down the details of every phone call that comes in. "And how long are they lasting? Are you getting a pain now? Good, keep breathing, that's it."

The woman on the other end of the phone is definitely contracting then.

"Have you had any loss down below? Any

blood or water? Not yet. Okay, that's fine. And it's your second baby, your husband said. Thirty-nine weeks?"

There's a slight pause whilst the woman answers and Chloe makes a note of the rest of the details.

"Any problems that we should know about? No. Okay. And you feel like you need to come in now? Yes, that's fine, Elizabeth. Do you have your notes there? I'll need your hospital number and address, so we can get your file. Great, thanks."

The ward clerk is already on her feet and walking to take the details from Chloe so that she can collect Elizabeth's main file. All patients have hand-held maternity notes so that they can carry them personally, but we also have a central file containing all of the patients' hospital records here on site.

Chloe comes into the staff room, and announces, "Elizabeth Foster, term, second baby, on her way in. All normal so far. Contracting every four minutes. Membranes intact. Violet."

I don't expect to hear my name and I splutter my tea. Luckily, I don't splash it over my uniform.

"Can you prepare a room for her, please?"

"Sure." I hold back my grin, but I share a quick glance with Jade. She makes a thumbs up sign. I lean to put my mug down on the table.

"Finish that first," Chloe says. "She'll be quarter of an hour, minimum, and you might not get the chance for another drink once she's here."

"I hope not!" I say. I expect that once I have qualified as a midwife and delivery suite shifts become routine, I will be less enthusiastic about the prospect of six hours on my feet without a brew. Today, I want to care for this woman in labour. I want to support Elizabeth and her husband, and I want to finally see a birth.

True to Chloe's estimate, the ward's door buzzer sounds twenty minutes later. Elizabeth's husband speaks into the intercom and Chloe lets them in. Jade looks at me.

"Ready?" she says.

"Absolutely!" I reply.

We walk down the corridor to meet the couple. Elizabeth has made it about six feet into the ward and has had to stop due to getting a contraction.

"Hi," Jade says. "Elizabeth?"

Her husband replies for her. "Hi. I'm Richard." He hands his wife's notes over to Jade and returns to leaning over by her side.

"We'll wait for this contraction to go and then get you into your room."

Elizabeth manages a nod.

"Was that a strong one?" Jade asks, once Elizabeth starts to straighten up.

"They all are now," she says. She is trying to

smile, despite her pain.

"Okay. Let's get you to your room. This is Violet, she is a student midwife, working with me today. Do you mind if she watches?"

"I don't mind if everyone in the hospital watches, I just want to get this baby out now."

I can't help but let out a little laugh as we open the door into the delivery room. I'm not sure that I would be able to keep my sense of humour if I were in labour, and it makes me like Elizabeth instantly.

Jade checks Elizabeth's vitals, listens to the baby's heartbeat and runs through the same questions that Elizabeth answered over the phone. How often are the contractions? How long do they last? How is she coping with the pain?

The pregnancy has been routine, and last time around Elizabeth had a straightforward delivery.

"I only had gas and air," she says. "I thought I was going to need an epidural. I was ready to have just about anything and everything, but it wasn't all that bad."

"And this time? How do you feel?" Jade asks.

"I'm okay so far."

Richard joins in. "The contractions have been getting more painful though. She's gripping my hand harder now."

Jade nods. "Let us know if you do need anything.

The gas and air is right here if you want it." She points to the tubing attached to a mouthpiece, waiting by the bed.

"I need this baby to come out, that's what I need." As Elizabeth speaks, another contraction grips her. She bends over, pushing her hands into the mattress. Richard stands by her side and place his hand over hers.

"You are doing great, Liz," he says.

"It. Doesn't. Feel. Great." She speaks the words as she tries to control her breathing.

As she reaches the peak of her contraction, she lets out a guttural groaning noise. Jade's expression changes immediately.

"Do you need to push?" she asks.

I'm amazed at how she can deduce that from the nature of the noise coming from Elizabeth.

"I need to poo. I need to go to the toilet."

"Okay, Elizabeth. After this contraction I am going to listen to baby's heartbeat, and then, if you don't mind, I want to quickly examine you and find out what's happening. I think you might be getting on in labour."

"I need the toilet," she says again.

Jade explains, "I think it might be baby's head pushing down that is making you feel like that. Have you been to the toilet recently?"

"She went at home, before we came out," Richard

says.

"Is it okay if I examine you quickly, and then you can pop to the toilet if you need to?"

Elizabeth shuffles out of her leggings, and clambers onto the bed whilst Jade washes her hands.

"Get my nightie out, Rich. Not the one with the bear on, that's for after. The striped one, get that. Thanks, love."

Jade speaks to me whilst Elizabeth gets changed. "I won't ask if you can repeat the examination this time, Violet. I think she is ready to push, and we won't have much time. I might need you to get me a delivery trolley. You remember where everything is?"

On our quiet shift yesterday, Jade showed me where everything is kept, and luckily, I paid attention. I nod. "Sure."

"Looks like you are finally going to see a birth."

Jade sits at the side of the bed next to Elizabeth with her gloves on.

"Okay, just relax and let your legs fall apart and I will be as quick as I can," she says.

Elizabeth has clearly been through this before, as she drops her legs apart and holds onto Richard's hand as Jade examines her.

"Yes, you are fully dilated," Jade says. "Baby's head is well down. Are you getting a contraction now?"

Elizabeth's voice changes as she squeaks, "Yes!"

"I'm going to keep still, alright. Keep breathing. Let me know if you feel like you want to push," Jade says. She turns to me and says, "Violet, get the trolley, please."

I pull the delivery pack from the cupboard and get everything ready on the trolley, just as Jade showed me yesterday.

"I need to pooh!" Elizabeth yells.

"You need to push," Jade says, much more softly. "Hold your breath and push down into your bottom."

I wheel the trolley next to Jade so that she can reach everything that she needs.

"That's brilliant, Elizabeth," I say.

"Keep it coming," Jade tells her.

Elizabeth lets go of her breath and inhales deeply again.

"That's it, Elizabeth. Use all of your contraction to push now. Push against that pain." Jade's voice is so calm and reassuring.

"Is it coming?" Richard asks. He's up next to her head but craning down to see if he can catch sight of anything below.

"I can feel baby moving when you push. You're doing really well. See if you can get three big pushes in with every contraction, and baby will soon be here."

Elizabeth closes her eyes and takes a few deep

breaths between contractions.

Jade points at the heartrate monitor, and I press the transducer gently against Elizabeth's abdomen. The machine pounds out a solid, steady heart rate of a hundred and twenty beats per minute.

"That sounds perfect," Jade says.

"It's coming again," Elizabeth says.

"Alright, you know what to do. Take a big breath in and push right down into your bottom. Let's get baby moving."

I stand at the bottom of the bed, next to Jade, and watch. As Elizabeth pushes, the birth canal gapes open slightly, and I can see my first glimpse of the baby's head.

"I can see your baby. You're pushing so well."

"Keep going, Elizabeth."

"Well done, Liz."

With the second push of the contraction, the baby moves even closer towards being born. I can see a five-centimetre diameter of the top of his head now. This is a lot quicker than I thought it would be.

"Nearly there, that's it."

When she pushes for the third time, the baby's head is almost bursting from the birth canal, and as the contraction ends, the head remains in sight.

"That stings," she says. "Can you get it out?"

"Soon you can get your baby out," Jade says. "I'm going to get you to pant with your next contraction, and let your uterus do the work. We're going to take it nice and slowly, and try to make sure you don't tear. Concentrate on panting, and listen to my voice, okay?"

"Okay," Elizabeth says. She sounds breathless. I wonder how it feels to be so close to giving birth, and to have the baby's head pushing against you like that.

The contraction soon starts to build, and as it does, baby's head slowly moves forwards.

"Pant, now. Pant."

Elizabeth takes tiny, short breaths and pants them out. Jade's hand is on the baby's head, controlling it as it crowns.

"Nearly there. Keep panting, keep going."

"Shit!" Elizabeth shouts as her baby's head is born.

"It's okay. You're alright. Baby's head is out now. You're nearly there. Just relax, wait for the next contraction now."

Richard hands his wife the plastic tumbler and she takes a quick sip of water.

Jade is reaching her finger into the birth canal, feeling around the baby's neck in case the cord is wrapped around it.

When the contraction builds, she tells Elizabeth, "Push now. Let's get baby out."

Elizabeth gives one huge shove, and Jade assists

the baby up and out of the birth canal, and into the warm delivery room.

"There you are," she says. "You were amazing."

She takes a quick look at the baby and then passes him up towards his parents.

It all happened so quickly. Elizabeth was controlled and calm, and now, as I watch her look at her newborn baby with tears in her eyes, I can't help letting out a few tears of my own.

Chapter Twenty-Five

Even though I still have the stress of the OSCE resit hanging over me, once I have finally seen a baby being born, I feel like something has changed. I was already enthusiastic, of course, this is what I have wanted to do for as long as I can remember, but being at the birth has given me an extra push. No pun intended. I can't wait until I can be the one holding out my hands to receive a baby into the world.

I feel like I am settling into university life. Even though I haven't taken any professional support for my anxiety, I feel lighter, more able to cope with whatever life throws at me. It seems I'm not the only one to notice this.

"You're full of the joys of spring," Luke says.

He finally caved and agreed to chip in with the table and chairs for the garden. It's looking great out here. Zoe and I have strung some outdoors fairy lights around the trellis against the wall, and Luke helped us to set up a bird table. At first, I shook out the crumbs from the bottom of the bags when we finished our loaves, but the more birds came to the table, the more I wanted to give. I've started making an extra slice of toast in the mornings just so I can pretend that I can't manage it and bring it out here for our feathered visitors.

Today Luke is taking the role of head chef. We've got a few sausages and burgers and a disposable barbeque on the go. It would be difficult not to be full of those joys today.

"Things are going pretty well right now," I tell him. "Delivery suite has been great; I've passed all of my written assignments so far. All I have to do now is –" I leave the sentence hanging. We have an unspoken agreement in the house that we won't mention my OSCE. Not until I am ready to talk about the resit, anyway. It's getting closer; I've been reading every night, trying to take in everything I need to so that I can pass this time. I have got to start thinking about something else.

It seems to have become cloudier since I started to let my mind focus on my exam. When we came into the garden there was bright sunshine. Zoe is wearing a yellow strappy dress and these amazing cork wedge sandals that she picked up in town last week. I'm, as always, rather less glamourous in a floral sundress that I have owned since I was sixteen. There's a small hole on the hem where the stitching has come loose, but I figure that no one is going to look closely enough to see it. Zoe knows it's there anyway.

Zoe's hair is pinned up into a chunky top-bun that looks effortless, but I know that she spends about half an hour achieving that look. She's sitting next to Luke as he flips the sausages, drinking Budweiser straight from the bottle. I used to think that Luke must feel like a third wheel being around the two of us, but now sometimes it feels like I am the piggy in the middle.

It's May bank holiday. The end of the month; the end of my delivery suite placement. There are four weeks in uni coming up. In less than two weeks time I will be resitting my OSCE.

It seems that no matter how hard I try to keep smiling and not think about it, the resit creeps into my thoughts.

A large wet splat falls onto the concrete in front of me, and I look up at the sky. Above, where there had been clear skies, is now a heavy grey blanket of cloud.

"Rain," I say flatly.

"You sure?" Zoe says. I don't think she even noticed that the sun had gone in.

I hold out my hand and let a few thick droplets of water pad down onto my palm.

There's a loud crash of thunder, and the sky opens.

"I am now," I say.

"Sod it." Luke puts the tongs down onto the tea towel by his side. My mind is so used to thinking midwifery thoughts that for a moment I picture them as forceps. I haven't seen them used in practice yet, but Jade let me hold some. They are strictly for the doctors to use, and I am relieved that I won't ever have that responsibility.

"Are we going in then?" Zoe is up on her feet, holding her cardigan over her head.

"Go on. I'll bring this indoors. Or I'll bring the food inside anyway." Luke makes a shooing motion with his hands, and the two of us push the door and go back into the kitchen.

Although I know it's a ridiculous thought, a part of me thinks for the flash of a second that I caused the weather to turn by thinking about my exam. I was happy and smiling and we were all having a great time, until my mind started to wander. I am not superstitious, but after bottling it in the last exam I feel somehow cursed. I said it was ridiculous.

"What's up?" Zoe says.

The two of us sit at the kitchen table, waiting for Luke to gather up the food from outside and bring it in.

"Nothing."

I can see him sliding the burgers off the grill onto a plate.

"Sure," she says. "I know it's not just the fact that we can't sit outside and eat our burnt food. Is it me?"

"What? Why would it be you?"

"Talking to Luke. I mean, am I talking to him too much and not talking to you?"

This has come out of nowhere. It's been six weeks since we came back here after Easter, and as far as I can tell Zoe has still not made her move. The two of them seem no closer to being together than they did before the Christmas holidays.

"Do you think you were?" I ask.

"So, you do," she says. "You do think that."

"Not at all. I didn't say that. What I mean is, do you feel like you are talking to him too much? Is that how you feel?"

"I don't know," she says. "At first, maybe. I get so self-conscious now. Like I want to impress him, or say the right thing, or at least not say the wrong thing. I feel like I am waiting for something to happen."

He's putting the sausages into a pile, waving one hand over his head in a futile attempt to bat away the falling rain.

"Do you think it's time to make something happen?"

She waves her hands in a dramatic shrug. "I don't want to rush things. I don't want to spoilt things happening naturally."

"This is what you said before Easter, and you were mortified when you thought you had lost him."

"It's not like he is out every night looking for women. He spends his evenings either with us or with the lads, and Raj, Flo and Damon are hardly womanisers."

If there's one thing that can distract me from thinking about my exam it's Zoe's prevaricating. I have often wondered if one of the reasons that I wanted a job in a caring profession is that while I am helping and supporting other people, I don't have time to worry about myself. I don't stress out and panic while I am focussing on being there for others. It's only when I stew on my own problems that they start to eat away at me. Anxiety can only hurt me because it overpowers me; it consumes my thoughts, replacing everything else.

Zoe picks up her bottle and picks at the label. I guess she is trying not to think about the thing that is stressing her out too. Actually telling Luke how she feels will be a massive step, I understand that.

"All I am saying is that I think you should be sure about what you want. And if you are sure, then don't let him get away."

She nods wordlessly and tips her head in the direction of the door to alert me to Luke coming through. Each of his hands is carrying a plate piled high with the food he was cooking.

"That went well," he says.

Luke grins, and I can almost hear Zoe sigh next to me. His hair is plastered to his head now, and his t-shirt is clinging to his chest.

He puts the food down on the countertop then he

says, "I'd better dry up and get changed. I guess we can cook this here and just pretend we are having a barbie."

Zoe pushes her chair back and gets to her feet. "I'll put the oven on and stick these in. You go and sort yourself out."

He reaches out to ruffle her hair, and then stops awkwardly, his hand in mid-air as he realises it's a tough job with her bun pinned up as it is. Instead he ends up patting her gently and she taps her hand against his wet chest in a mock 'get off me' gesture.

Not that I know anything about relationships, but I am fairly certain that this is flirtatious behaviour on both sides. Awkward and badly co-ordinated, but flirtatious all the same.

Chapter Twenty-Six

My placement ends on the last day of May, and I have the weekend blocked out to focus on revision. I may have tried to stop myself from getting worked up about the exam until now, but the circle that I have drawn on my calendar is glaring out at me from the moment I get out of bed.

The plan is this: Zoe and Luke are going into town for the morning. Whilst they are out, I am going to go through everything I have learned about my scenarios. When they come back, Luke is going to play act the patient, and Zoe is going to be the tutor. Of course, I asked Zoe to be the patient again, but she had this gem of an idea.

"Someone should watch to check you are saying all the right things, covering all the bases and that," she said.

It made sense.

"And if someone else is there apart from me the stress of the situation will be more real for you. You're hardly going to be shitting yourself if it's just the two of us. You need to practice how you are going to behave, not just what you are going to say."

That made even more sense.

What I should have done is call up one of the girls from my class, or Simon of course, and ask them to come over and help me. I could have done that.

Zoe has been so helpful though, and I kind of want to do this for her. I want her to see how much she helps me. Not just by supporting me and letting me practice with her, but her general presence. She is a calming influence. I only wish she could be there at the exam with me.

I was going to ask one of my course mates to come and be a mock patient for me, but Luke overheard Zoe and I talking, and that's how I ended up with a six-foot-tall man with stubble as my pretend pregnant woman.

I make coffee and then sit at my desk and focus. This is my last chance to nail it before the test this week. I would rather have had the exam first thing Monday morning instead of having to get through the week of lectures.

I read through all of the sections in Myles Midwifery that relate to the possible scenarios. I check through my lecture notes and flick through the slides on the virtual learning environment. I turn away from the desk and speak into the empty room, telling my bed and the door what I would do in each of the potential role play situations. The thing is, I know all of the information that I need to know. I have the facts indelibly imprinted in my brain. It feels like basic, fundamental knowledge to me now. When I first stood outside the skills lab waiting to go in to take the exam, my mind was blank. Now I can't imagine everything that I have learned by heart being so difficult to access from my brain. It's not that I don't know what to do or what to say. The problem is staying calm for long enough to be able to do and say it.

When the others get home, I run downstairs to meet them. Zoe hands me a takeaway cup from Blackheath's containing a still-hot latte.

"We went there last," she smiles.

"You went there without me!" I say.

"I don't even like coffee, but that's a great place." Luke is carrying two bags of groceries and he squeezes past to get to the kitchen.

"Anything exciting happen?" I ask when he is out of earshot. Zoe shakes her head, and I shrug and smile. I don't know what else to say right now.

"How did you get on with the cramming?" she says.

"I think I have stuffed all of the info into my tiny brain," I say. "Now I need to find the secret formula for getting it out again when I need it…without letting anxiety mess it up for me."

Luke rests his hand firmly on my shoulder.

"I'm ready to be your patient," he says. "The things we do for friends, eh?"

"Thanks," I say. "I appreciate this. I owe you

one."

He smiles. "When I need someone to act as a client for an accountancy role play, I will let you know."

Somehow, he always manages to lighten the atmosphere. I can see why Zoe likes him. Fortunately, we have never been attracted to the same type, but I am glad that he is my friend.

We go into the sitting room to run through our role plays, or at least Zoe and Luke go in, and I stand in the hallway. It's the anxiety that I have to get over. The worst part for me will be standing in the corridor, waiting to go in for my exam, taking the card, and getting started. When I get going I will be able to trick my mind into thinking that I am in a real clinical setting, I know I will, and when that happens, my anxiety won't be able to hurt me.

I asked Zoe to let me wait in the hall for a couple of minutes before we start. I want to feel the build-up, and train myself to cope with it. Even here, at home, knowing that I am going into my own living room to work through a scenario with my two friends, my pulse is pounding. The bottom line is that I know how important this exam is. I know what is at stake. I practice slowing my breath, focusing my thoughts. I feel that nervous twitch gripping my body, the creeping cold of anxiety thundering through my veins. I let it build. I let myself feel the anxiety that I know I will feel in six days' time when I have to do this for real.

And then

I let it go.

I breathe deeply.

I concentrate on the tension in my body.

I focus on my heartrate, commanding myself to be calm, to relax.

Negative thoughts flood my brain. I can't do it. I'm going to fail again. I'm going to fail the year.

And I think

No.

Not this time.

I can do this.

Those four words, "I can do this", sound so similar to the words that I have told myself so many times before. Until now, it has always been the reverse, the negative. I can't do this. I can't.

Not this time.

I know that this isn't the end of anxiety for me, but as I push open the door, it isn't fear that I feel, it is self-confidence.

I pick up a card from the coffee table, and I run through the scenario.

I can do this.

Chapter Twenty-Seven

If I was worried about the week dragging, I need not have been. Friday morning comes around in a flash. There's only one other student resitting apart from me. No waiting around for my turn, no time to stand in the corridor letting the anxiety bubble within me.

Rachel comes to let me in.

"Good morning, Violet. Leave your bag by the door and, when you're ready, go and choose your first scenario. Bridget Brody is the second marker today. I don't think you know her, but she will be leading one of your second-year modules."

Second year. If I make it through.

I nod, silently, take a deep breath and go through the door. I allow myself one look over to where the other lecturer and the actress are sitting.

The woman playing the part of the patient isn't the same as the one who was here last time. I'm thankful for that. I don't know if I could have handled seeing her again after I messed up so badly before. The tutors have seen other students in other years struggle through this exam, but having a stranger, someone from the outside world, see me like that was mortifying.

There are six cards face-down on the table, just like last time. However, this time I don't spend minutes trying to decide which card to take. This time, I reach out, let my hand fall upon whichever scenario fate decides to give me, and I turn it over immediately.

Antenatal. Okay. That's got to be good. The woman is thirty-six weeks pregnant, and I am seeing her for an antenatal appointment. It's her first baby, everything has been normal so far, but today her blood pressure is 145/100.

High blood pressure. I can do this. I close my eyes for a few moments. I'm trying to imagine myself in the antenatal clinic, trying to picture Stacey, way back in those first weeks, showing me the basics. Blood pressure checks are routine. Knowing what to do when the results are abnormal is a basic midwifery skill. I can do this.

I open my eyes, focus upon the woman, and walk over to where she and my two tutors are waiting.

Rachel checks the scenario that I chose and shows it to the woman and the other tutor. Both of them nod.

"I have some additional information here for you," Rachel says. She reaches onto the table beside her and hands me some paperwork. There's a partially completed pregnancy record, and a chart that we refer to as a MEOWS chart. It's nothing to do with cats; it's a Modified Early Obstetric Warning Score, used on maternity wards to record vital signs and physiological observations. They are similar to the notes and charts that I have been working with on my placements. They feel recognisable and the familiarity is comforting.

I can feel my own pulse pounding, and my blood pressure may well be as high as the subject in the scenario by now, but I breathe, and I focus. Even though my skin is prickling, and my mind is racing, I bring myself back to the present moment.

Rachel has a concerned expression; perhaps she thinks I am going to mess this up again. We both know what is at stake. I can't fail.

"Are you ready to begin?" she asks.

I suck in a breath, look at the scenario, and at the paperwork in my hand, and then nod.

"Yes. Let's go."

As soon as I start the mock-assessment of the patient my instincts take over. I can feel my heart beating double time, thudding against my chest wall, but as soon as I become aware of it, I concentrate on slowing my breathing, calming myself, focussing on the scenario. There's no room for self-doubt. I have to give this everything I have got.

I greet the actress as though she is really my patient, and I carry out the observations just as I would if I were with Stacey out in community. As I am talking to the woman, I feel my fear slipping away. The more I concentrate on what I am doing the less chance my anxiety has to wheedle its way in.

I write in the notes, detailing and documenting everything to the letter. I know exactly what I should do, and I do it.

I'm sure that the lecturers are meant to remain impartial, but I am aware of Rachel smiling at me and nodding as I fill in the MEOWS chart and sign my name.

When I have completed the second scenario and it is time to leave, I know that I have done my best and I am as confident as I can be that I have passed this time. I have studied and I have rehearsed, but most of all I have learned something about myself. I have learned to listen to my body, to listen to my mind, but more than that, I have learned to not always believe what they tell me.

I can do this. I can.

Chapter Twenty-Eight

With the OSCE behind me there are six weeks left of term. I have two assignments to hand in, and a four-week placement on the antenatal ward. I already feel like I am starting to wind down for the year. I won't actually get my OSCE results until the end of the month, but I don't need to see the number on the screen to know what I need to know. I have passed. Rachel as much as told me that before I left the skills lab. I guess she didn't want me to have to go through any more stress about the exam. I can forget about the OSCE… until we have our second next year. Right now, I feel invincible.

Zoe has placements until the end of term. Apparently it's a good time for her to be out in school. The Year Elevens are finishing their exams, the Year Tens are excited about coming back for their final year of GCSEs. I don't remember being quite as thrilled as Zoe describes it, but I am feeling something of that buzz now. I have made it through the year; I can't wait to start again in October. Now that I have made it through the resit, I can relax and enjoy the rest of term.

My antenatal placement begins at the start of July. From the outset, I feel like I am winding down towards the two months of summer holidays. I'm not sure what I am going to do with myself for all of those weeks away from here. Tangiers Court feels like home now. That said, it's not a certainty yet that we will return to the house that we have come to love.

I am sitting on the sofa, with Zoe next to me, her legs stretched across my lap, Luke is on one of the armchairs. It's a standard evening here: television, coffee, and conversation.

"Not that I don't want a holiday," Zoe says, "but being back with my parents is going to be weird."

"Your parents are down the road," Luke smiles. "You could go home every night if you wanted to. If you think that is going to be weird, try spending the summer in Leeds."

"Sounds exotic," I say. I've never been any further north than Bristol, so in a way Yorkshire is exotic to me.

When we first came here I thought I would be on the phone to my mum all the time, driving her nuts by wanting to go home every weekend. She and I were a team, the two of us, through all of the crappy times she had with my dad. Leaving home and coming here though, I feel like it's given us both the space we needed. Mum's socialising now, always telling me about the book club she's joined or the friends she is meeting up with from work. She never did any of that when I was at home. Perhaps I am going to be in the way when I go back.

"Do you girls have anything exciting planned?" Luke asks.

That phrase 'you girls' instantly makes me think of my father, and the way he used to talk down to Mum and me. It feels like I have been burying my thoughts of home and of the past few years while I have been here, kind of out of sight and out of mind. Now that I am thinking about going home, they are all flooding back.

"Spend some time with my mum," I say.

"Yeah, and catch up with some of our friends who are off at uni all over the place, hopefully," Zoe adds.

There aren't that many people that I am bothered about seeing, but Zoe always had more friends than I did. She likes to keep in touch, whereas I tend to let go. I'm happy spending my time with Zoe, I don't feel the need to keep up with anyone else. I wonder if Luke lives somewhere else next year whether I will lose touch with him too.

"Are you planning on living with the lads next year?" Zoe asks. She slips in the question like it means nothing to her, but I know that it means so much.

He shrugs and takes a drink from his mug. "Haven't thought about it," he says. He doesn't make eye contact when he speaks. I wonder if he is telling the truth.

Zoe flashes me a look, as if looking for backup, but I really don't know what to say. Her plan of waiting for things to happen between them doesn't seem to be getting her anywhere. They obviously get on well, and I am sure that he flirts with her just as much as she does with him, but perhaps that's just the kind of person he is. If she isn't going to make a move, maybe nothing will ever happen.

"We haven't started looking yet," I say. "I'd like to stay here, I think."

I try to make it sound casual, but Zoe and I have spoken about it at length. Our ideal scenario sees Luke, Zoe and I staying at Tangiers Court, and the fourth bedroom staying empty. Not that I wouldn't like to see some geeky-but-gorgeous guy move in with us, but I think I would rather have the extra space in the house than the extra complication in my life.

Luke nods silently and focuses on the television. As we have been talking throughout most of the episode that's playing it feels like he is avoiding the topic rather than actually watching the programme. Zoe chose this one; it's some cookery competition where the guests have to try and make their creations look, and taste, like the ones that a professional has made earlier. They always come out looking like abominations, but that's what makes it fun. I can identify with those bakers, and a part of me probably identifies with the cakes too: always trying to be what I am supposed to be, but never quite getting there.

The three of us sit without saying another word until the end of the episode. Then Luke gets to his feet.

"Anyone want another drink or anything while I'm up?"

Zoe and I both shake our heads.

"Be back in a minute then. Start the next one if you want."

He leaves the room, and walks down the hall to the bathroom. I watch him go into the room and close the door, and then I speak to Zoe.

"Are you going to say something, or –"

"I don't want to spoil things," she says in a hushed tone. "This is all so perfect. I feel like if I say something and he's not into me, I'm going to mess everything up."

I tighten my lips and frown. "It's up to you, but what if this is it? What if he moves out next month? You'll hardly see him. You might never see him."

"You really think he isn't going to stay here? You saw him, just as clearly as I did. He says he hasn't thought about it, but I think it's pretty obvious…"

Luke's footsteps pad back down the hallway; I put

my finger to my lips to hush Zoe.

He settles back into his chair.

"I'll message the landlord and see if this place is even available for next year," I say. "Just let us know when you decide what you want. I mean, what you want to do."

I feel Zoe give me a little kick of her leg against my thigh and Luke looks over at me.

"Sure," he says.

I'm not convinced that trying to be subtle is going to prompt either of them to make a move, but sitting on the side lines, watching them, I feel like I have to do something.

Chapter Twenty-Nine

I settle into my antenatal ward placement easily. I think, in part, it's because I don't have the worry of university work to think about. So far, I have had the option of following the night shift pattern of my mentors or plumping to stick to daytime and working with someone else. With only two weeks left of the academic year, all my coursework handed in and nothing planned on my social calendar it seems like as good a time as any to volunteer for the night shift.

I can't imagine that much exciting happens on the antenatal ward at night. Most of the women with pregnancy complications have the same sleep-wake patterns as anyone else. By the time we have taken handover at half past eight, conducted the routine observations, circled the ward with medications and again with bedtime drinks and snacks, almost everyone is settling down to sleep.

By ten o'clock the lights are dimmed, and my mentor, the second and only other midwife on shift, Caroline, and I are sitting in the midwives' office, mugs of tea in our hands.

It's a good opportunity for me to go through my PAD, making sure it's up to date, and having Becky sign off some of my competencies.

A call bell buzzes out from the darkened bays.

"I'll go," I offer. Becky nods, and I get up and walk out into the ward.

I have to look for where the call is coming from. The first bay to my left is dark and silent. In the second, one of the women has her lamp on, reading a Kindle, but she smiles as I pass by. At the bottom of the ward, I find two women sitting together; Jackie, a third-time mum with high blood pressure that we are monitor is rubbing her hand on the lower back of Carla, a primip who came in leaking fluid this evening. It looks like her waters have definitely broken, but up until now she wasn't getting any pains.

I silence the buzzer.

"Are you okay? What's happening?"

Jackie speaks. "She's getting contractions. She didn't want to bother you, but I told her to buzz. They are regular now. Every three minutes."

Carla nods, but says nothing. She's eighteen, single, and she looks terrified.

"It's alright," I say. "It's going to be alright. When did they start?"

Jackie starts to answer, but I nod towards Carla.

"I don't know," she says. "They started getting stronger, more regular after I lay down. I tried to ignore it and go to sleep, but they're…"

Her sentence is interrupted by the onset of another

contraction. Jackie runs her hand in circles on Carla's back.

"Can I feel?" I ask. She nods, and I place my hand, softly, onto the top of her uterus, palpating the contraction. I feel her abdomen stiffen beneath my palm, the tight grip of the contraction hard against my hand. "Breathe slowly, deeply. In and out. Nice and easy. Okay, that's it." She is doing a great job of staying calm, but I can see the discomfort in her face.

"Do you need some pain relief?"

She shakes her head briskly and resolutely.

As soon as the contraction has passed, she takes a few more deep breaths and then says "I wanted to go without. I don't want anything."

"Okay," I say. "You can ask for some any time that you want to." She nods. "How about a couple of paracetamol for a start? It sometimes helps with the early pains."

"No." She says it sharply, and then adds, "Thank you."

"That's fine." I say. "Can I have a quick listen to your baby's heartbeat, please? Check how he or she…"

"He," she smiles.

"Check how he is getting on with these contractions."

"Sure," she says.

Jackie stands up, but Carla grabs out for her hand and pulls her back. "Please stay," she says.

Jackie looks to me for approval and I nod. "Of course."

Carla lays back so that I can palpate her abdomen and find the position of the baby. His head is well down. He's lying with his back to Carla's side. Everything is normal. As I am about to put the fetal heart transducer onto her abdomen she starts to have another contraction.

"Would you feel better sitting?" I pull her up, and Jackie resumes her support. I unobtrusively listen in to the baby's heart rate while Carla breathes through the contraction.

It's slower than it should be.

Instead of the rapid thudding that I should hear, the heartbeat thuds away at around a hundred beats per minute. I try not to show my concern, and I reach up to palpate Carla's pulse rate, to check that it's not her heartbeat that I am auscultating.

As the contraction eases up, the heart rate speeds back to a normal rate. One hundred and twenty-five beats per minute. That's more like it.

Carla is sitting on the edge of the bed again now. That dip in the heart rate. It isn't normal. I need to fetch Becky to listen and check her over. What do I do next? It feels like the OSCE all over again, but this time for real. I don't panic though. There's not a shred of anxiety.

"Carla. Baby's heartbeat slowed down a little bit when you had your contraction then. I'm going to pop and get my supervisor to have a listen, okay?"

I don't want to start talking about all of the reasons that a baby's heart rate might drop. It could be position, it could be compression of the umbilical cord, there could be something more serious at work. I don't have the knowledge or confidence yet to make this judgement, so I do exactly what I should do, I ask Carla to lie on her left side, and I hurry to fetch Becky.

My supervisor comes immediately and confirms the details that I have gathered.

The contractions are strong and regular.

Becky talks to Carla in a reassuring tone. "If it's okay with you, I want to check how far dilated you are, and listen in to baby. If you're in labour, we'll get you upstairs to delivery suite. If your baby's heartrate keeps dropping with the contractions, you're going to need to be transferred up so we can keep an eye on him and get one of the doctors to find out what's going on."

"Do you want me to go?" Jackie asks.

Carla shakes her head. She looks scared, but she lies back on the bed so that Becky can examine her.

I don't ask whether I can practice my skills too.

It's not the right time.

Becky washes her hands and puts on her gloves. She sits at the side of the bed and slicks her fingers with lubricating jelly.

"Bring your legs up and let them flop apart at the knees," Becky says.

Carla keeps her eyes focussed on Jackie, up the top end of the bed.

"Okay, okay. Let me know if you get a contraction and I will keep still." Becky gently slides her fingers into the birth canal, and there are a few seconds where a look of concentration fixes upon her face, as she feels for the cervix. "Are you starting to get a contraction now?" she asks.

Carla nods and starts to breathe deeply, blowing out her exhalations. Her left hand is gripping Jackie's, her right is grasping the bottom sheet.

"Are you getting any pressure in your bottom?" Becky asks. My eyes widen at the question. Is she this far on?

Carla frantically bobs her head. "Yes. I think I need to go to the toilet."

"It's baby's head pressing down on your bottom. It's okay." Becky nods towards the heart rate monitor in my hand and then to Carla's abdomen, and I take the hint. The heart rate is still dipping.

"Baby is on his way," Becky says. "The heart rate is dropping because he is getting squashed on his way down. Sometimes the cord can get trapped a little bit so it's more difficult for baby to get all of the oxygen he needs." She withdraws her fingers. "Violet, ask Caroline to call the junior obstetrician; tell her what's happening and bring a delivery pack."

"Don't I need to go upstairs?" Carla says.

"I think you are too far on for that. We'll get a doctor down, just in case. And I need to pop you on the monitor. Baby's heartbeat is picking up between contractions but…"

I'm on my way to the office so I don't hear the rest of the explanation. This wasn't what I expected for my first night shift. Caroline is looking through a magazine at the desk and looks up sharply as I run through everything that I must remember to tell her.

"Thanks, Violet," she says. She picks up the phone to call the obstetrician.

On the way back to Carla's bed, I pick up the delivery pack from the storeroom. Should I ask Becky if I can deliver the baby? I've seen my quota; I could do this. On the antenatal ward though? There's not a proper delivery bed. These are the flat, regular hospital type, they don't have electronic risers to lift the backrests, they don't come apart in the middle so that you can sit between the woman's legs as you prepare to catch the baby. Are those things necessary?

I wheel a trolley over and start to open the

delivery pack for my supervisor.

"I can see the top of baby's head when you get the contractions," Becky says, giving Carla a reassuring smile. She's managed to link the cardiotocograph machine up to measure the heart rate and contractions, and I can see the short, sharp deceleration of the heart rate on the tracing with the contraction. As soon as the contraction ends, the heart rate picks back up to a regular, variable beat within normal limits.

"Caroline is letting the doctors know, and she's told sister on delivery suite too."

Becky nods. "Thanks." She turns to Carla. "You're nearly there, okay? You're doing so well."

I'm amazed at how little noise Carla is making despite being so far advanced in labour. I don't think I would be able to be this quiet.

"Violet is at the end of her first year of training," Becky says, and I know what is coming next. I feel a flushed thrill through my body. "Would you mind if I supervised her to help you deliver your baby?"

Carla shakes her head. "No." My thrill thuds to a full stop but then she adds. "No. I don't mind."

I can't control my grin. I pull a pair of gloves from the bottom of the trolley, and quickly head to wash my hands so that I can prepare.

I set up the equipment, and Becky moves from the

edge of the bed to allow me to sit.

"It's not going to be much longer, Carla. Are you feeling that urge to push?"

"Yes. Really bad."

"When you get your next contraction, take a big deep breath in, and hold it. Use that to push right down into your bottom."

"I might poo myself." She laughs nervously.

"I think I pooed myself with both of mine," Jackie says. "They've seen it all before." She indicates Becky and me, and I smile.

"It's all normal. If you do, it means you must be pushing well. Try not to think about it. Definitely don't worry about it."

She doesn't have time to say anything else, because the next contraction starts.

"Big deep breath," I say. "And push. Hold it as long as you can. Perfect." The brown hair on top of the baby's head moves closer to me. I'm sitting back, watching the baby, watching Carla, watching the heartrate. No dip this time. I look at Becky and point to the monitor. She nods and makes a mark in Carla's notes.

"Well done, Carla, that's great. And again."

She grits her teeth and gives it everything she's got. All my focus is directed upon the present moment. I don't have any thoughts of my own feelings, all that exists in this instant is Carla, and her baby.

"One more push before your contraction ends," I tell her, and she does it. She pushes in one extended effort, and when she lets it go and flops back into the pillows the baby's head stays, more of it visible now.

Becky has a towel ready at the side of me. Before the next contraction starts, a head pops around the corner of the curtain around the bay.

"Hi, I'm on call tonight," the doctor says. "How are we doing?"

My supervisor turns to talk to him and fills him in on the details. He looks at the heart rate tracing and nods.

"Looks like baby is ready to come out, Carla," he says. "I'm going to stay here a little while, and see what's happening, but I think as long as you push him out soon everything is going to be fine."

Carla is in no position to have a conversation right now.

"Okay, Carla?" I say. "Everything is fine. You can do this. A few more pushes like the last ones when you get your next contraction. Are you comfortable? Do you need to sit up more?"

She has slouched a little in the bed, it's not so easy with these flat bases as it is with the beds on delivery suite to help her into a comfortable position.

"I'm okay," she breathes.

Another contraction starts.

"Go on, Carla," the doctor says. "Show me how well you can push."

I want to keep leading the delivery, but I feel less confident with the doctor and midwife both watching.

"That's it," I say. I start to get caught back up in the birth. "Perfect, Carla. Big breath. Push. Hold on to it, keep it coming. Amazing." I don't have to think of the words because they come out easily. She is amazing. This is amazing.

Three more tremendous pushes, and the baby's head is almost crowning. When Carla relaxes at the end of the contraction, I pat her on the hand to make sure I have her attention.

"Next time, I need you to give me a big push again, but I need you to listen to me carefully. Baby's head is nearly out, and I am going to tell you when to stop pushing, and just breathe in shallow, tiny pants like a dog, okay?" I demonstrate. "It's going to help baby to come out more slowly, so that you don't tear."

She nods quickly. "Okay," she says. "I need a drink."

Jackie passes her the plastic cup from the bedside unit. She takes a few quick sips, and then it is time to concentrate on one of the final contractions.

I have my fingers on the top of the baby's head now, flexing as I have seen done by the midwives before.

Becky leans over me, putting her hand over mine, feeling to make sure that I am doing everything as I should. "That's great," she whispers to me. "You're doing great. You okay?" I nod and smile and focus on Carla.

"Big push. And...okay stop pushing, just breathe now. Tiny breaths. Pant, pant, pant."

The baby's head moves slowly into my hand, and suddenly in one bursting movement, the whole head emerges from the birth canal.

"Head's out, Carla. Well done. Just relax now. Wait for the next contraction, and baby will be here."

The baby's face is all squashed up, his lips puckered, eyes tightly shut. He's covered in blood and fluid, and I gently reach down by the side of his neck, feeling for any sign of umbilical cord around his neck. I feel it. A shiny smooth loop wrapped around him.

"There's cord around his neck," I say to my supervisor.

"Slip your finger between the cord and his neck," she says, and I do it. "Good. Now slide it up and over his head. That's it."

It slides easily and I smile in relief. "No problem, Carla. That's probably what was upsetting him a little earlier."

The contraction comes more slowly this time, and it feels like an age that I am sitting, looking at the baby's head, waiting for the contraction that will bring the rest of the baby into the world. Finally, Carla grunts, and starts to push.

"Guide the shoulders, Violet," Becky reminds me.

I gently assist the baby through the last stages of his journey into the world. His shoulder passes easily beneath Carla's pelvic bone and with one last huge push, she becomes a mother.

A perfect, healthy baby boy lies on the towel in front of me. Pink, soft and a little goo-covered, but absolutely perfect.

I look up at Carla through the emotional tears that I can't hold back.

"Is he okay?" she asks.

"He is awesome." I wrap him loosely in the towel and pass him up so that she can press her son against her skin.

"Good work ladies," the doctor says. He signs his name on the CTG trace and backs out of the bed space.

"Well done, Carla," Becky says. She looks at me and mouths "Well done, Violet."

All I can do is grin. "I didn't do anything," I say. "It was all Carla."

Chapter Thirty

Catching the bus back to Tangiers Court the morning after my first night shift, I am barely able to keep my eyes open. It's only the last waves of excitement rippling through me that keep me focussed. The bus is hot and full; there are a mixture of hospital staff leaving work and making their way back home, to their beds, mostly as tired-looking as I am, and day workers heading into town for their nine-to-fives. I'll probably never know what it is like to live that life. I will always be heading to or from work at unsociable hours, waking up at six in the morning or six at night, working weekends when my friends are partying, putting in evening shifts when Zoe is at home watching television.

It strikes me that she might have already left for the day by the time I get back to the house. I need to sleep, but I want to spill out all the details about how I, Violet Cobham, have delivered a baby. It's a massive, emotional milestone, and I want to share it with Zoe.

I check my phone. It's nearly eight o'clock. Her first alarm will be going off on the hour; I'm sure it's not too early to text her.

I tap in a message

I did it! I delivered a baby!!!! xx

I'm about to press SEND when I change my mind.

I want to tell her in person. I want to see the look on her face when she hears my news.

I rest my head against the window, and smile to myself, and I don't care who sees me do it.

Ten minutes later I bundle through the front door, throw my keys into the bowl on the table and race up to her room.

"Zoe! Zoe! Zoe!" I sing the words as I take the stairs two at a time.

I burst in through her bedroom door and find her, still lying in bed. I can't stop myself though. I launch myself onto her and wrap her up in a huge hug.

"I delivered my first baby!"

Zoe lets out a whooping noise and throws her arms back around me.

The two of us lie side-by-side on her bed making excited sounds, while I try to share the whole story with her.

Luke is on his way downstairs, and he stops to pop his head into the room.

"Oh yes?" he says, with a smile. The two of us snuggled up on Zoe's bed must be quite a sight.

"She delivered a baby!" Zoe shrieks.

"Nice work, Violet," he says. "Do I get to join in the hug too?"

"Maybe not on my bed," Zoe says. I wink at her, and she starts to blush.

"Come on," I say, getting to my feet and reaching my arms towards him.

Zoe drags herself up and joins in, and we spend the next five minutes wrapped up in the best group hug that I have ever experienced.

The curtains in my room are thin, and the excitement pumping through me is intense. It's hard to get to sleep, but once Luke and Zoe have left for the day, I finally drift off.

By the time Zoe gets home at just before five I've slept a few hours, but probably not quite as many as I would have liked. As soon as I hear her, I sit up and throw my feet onto the floor.

"Zo!" I call out into the landing.

"Vi, Vi, Vi," she shouts as she runs up and throws herself into my room.

More quietly she asks, "is he home?"

I shake my head. "Just us."

She grabs hold of me and we hug again.

"You delivered a baby!" she says. "How amazing. Tell me all about it. I thought you were on antenatal. What happened?"

I stumble downstairs in my pyjamas and sit at the kitchen table with her. She makes her dinner and I have my breakfast. The future is going to be filled with days like this, but I can't imagine that any of them will be quite this exciting.

I didn't feel the tiniest trace of anxiety. I focused on Carla, on the baby, on what I had to do to make sure she had a positive, happy, safe delivery. That was all that mattered to me. It wasn't like I was running on autopilot, I'm far too inexperienced for that, but something powered me on, leading me through everything I had to remember, everything I had to do. If I was on autopilot, I might have parroted off the words that I thought I should say, but I didn't.

Everything about the birth was natural and easy, not just for Carla, but for me too. Becky supported me to do my best. I knew she was there, but she didn't intrude, she let me take the lead. I make a mental note to tell her tonight how much I appreciate that. The silent support meant so much.

It's getting towards the end of year, it will soon be time for the holidays, three long months before I return. Seeing a birth has been an amazing climax, but now I don't want the year to finish.

Chapter Thirty-One

I wrap up the final chapter of my first year as a student midwife with one last three-way meeting between my antenatal mentor and my link tutor. It's the last week of my placement. I'm flicking through my PAD, reading through the comments that I have left along the way and the notes made by my sign-off mentors.

It's amazing how much I have managed to pack into one year. Looking back to that first day in class, months ago when I walked into the lecture block. I hadn't even got my uniform. All I had was excitement, tinged with fear and apprehension, and laced with a little of that self-doubt that is my signature ingredient. But despite everything, the ups and downs of the year, I have made it through.

I finish my shift and Becky and I head into the office to meet with Deb.

"Good to see you, Violet. How has it been going?"

I'm all smiles. I've enjoyed every placement this year, but antenatal has turned out to be my favourite. Not necessarily because I got to deliver a baby, but I feel like I have had time here to talk to women, to spend time with them and make a difference to their experience. Isn't that what my motivation has always been?

"I love my antenatal placement," I tell her. "I

think I have learned a lot."

Becky nods. "It's been great having Violet here. The women have given a lot of positive feedback." I can feel my heart pounding, not with anxiety, not now. This is pride. This is the flip side of fear.

I have learned such a lot this year. Not just about starting to become a midwife, but also about myself, and about what I can achieve if I put my mind to it.

When I get back to Tangiers Court, Zoe runs to meet me. I can see from the look on her face that she has been waiting for me to get home.

"Did you get a text from the landlord?" Zoe asks. She's almost jumping up and down with excitement.

I did get the message. He wants to know whether we want to renew the contract for the next academic year. The house is available, it's up to us whether we stay. Tangiers Court feels like home now. It's ideally located for the bus ride to my placements, and not far for Zoe to travel to hers. Uni is a ten-minute walk. I can't imagine that we would be able to find anywhere better. It's roomy, comfortable and, well, it's our home. Of course, we want to stay.

"Yes! Good news! I'm so glad we get another year," I say.

"I love it here." She grins and takes both of my hands in hers. "I'm so glad we get to stay."

We jump up and down like excited kids. When

we settle back to our seats, I ask the million-dollar question. "What about Luke?"
She shrugs. "I haven't asked him yet. Has he said anything more about it? He hasn't said anything to me. He might have had enough of us. He might want to go and live with Rash, Florian and Damon." Her voice is an excited garble.

It's possible though. Just because we have lived together this year doesn't mean that he will necessarily want to keep living with us.

"I'll ask him," she says, and that seems like the most straightforward approach. "I want us to all stay here, to be just the way we are right now. I want to carry on doing placements, and, well, I don't really care about lectures, and I particularly don't care about assignments, but apart from that, I don't want anything to change. I want this. This here. Just this." The words spill out of her in a fast, furious deluge, and she stops at the end, breathless.

"Oh Zo. I want that too."
As I finish speaking, Luke's key turns in the lock and he calls in from the hall.

"Have you told him we are staying?"
Zoe looks at me, and beams.
Luke comes straight into the living room and sits down next to Zoe.

"We were just talking about it," Zoe says.
"Yeah, I thought you might prefer to move in with

the cool boys rather than hang around with us two for another year."

"As if I would choose to live with a bunch of accountants when I could be with you," he says.

I wonder if he always knew that he would stay, or whether he was waiting to see what happened with Zoe? Or whether his friends asked him to live with them? I really don't know.

"I'll check with Andrew if he is staying too." I laugh, and then I stop myself. "What if someone does move into that room next year? I mean, they must, someone has to move in, surely?"

"The landlord won't keep it empty for two years," Zoe says. "He must be losing a lot of money."

The thought hangs in the room like an unwanted visitor.

"He'll get used to us," Luke says. "Whoever moves in will have to take us as we are."

There will be less space, more sharing, and no one to act as a convenient excuse when we want to skip the washing up or order takeaway. Then again, if we hadn't moved into a multi-occupancy house, we would never have met Luke, and I'm sure that's a world that Zoe doesn't want to imagine. Who knows, perhaps the new housemate will turn out to be the man of my dreams. Who knows, maybe next year Zoe will finally get around to telling Luke how she feels.

Dear Reader,

Thank you for reading **"Life Lessons"**, book one in the **"Lessons of a Student Midwife"** series.

If you have enjoyed this book, please consider leaving a review on Amazon and/or Goodreads. Reviews help readers to discover books, and help authors to find new readers.

If you would like to find out more about new releases and special offers, including information about the rest of this series, please sign up to my mailing list. Visit **jerowney.com** for details.

Best wishes
J.E. Rowney

Printed in Great Britain
by Amazon